W9-ACR-980

THE SWEET SHORT GRASS

THE SWEET SHORT GRASS

PETER INCHBALD

ASBURY PARK PUBLIC LIBRARY
ASBURY PARK, NEW JERSEY

PUBLISHED FOR THE CRIME CLUB BY
DOUBLEDAY & COMPANY, INC.
GARDEN CITY, NEW YORK
1982

All of the characters in this book
are fictitious, and any resemblance
to actual persons, living or dead,
is purely coincidental.

Library of Congress Cataloging in Publication Data

Inchbald, Peter.
The sweet short grass.

(Crime Club)
I. Title.
PR6059.N3S9   1982   823'.914
                AACR2
ISBN 0-385-18255-4
Library of Congress Catalog Card Number 82–45359

First Edition in the United States of America

Copyright © 1982 by Peter Inchbald
All Rights Reserved
Printed in the United States of America

Without the help of numerous friends, acquaintances, and former strangers, I would have made worse jobs of both this and my earlier Franco Corti book. Some of you would rather not be mentioned, and to thank some individually would constitute name-dropping. So rather than pick and choose, I offer you this as a sort of collective dedication, with my thanks, my apologies if I have been a pest, and my hope that you have kept me not too far from the rails.

P.I.

CONTENTS

CHAPTER 1

A FRIENDLY RUSSIAN

It was Frank Short's first case as a detective chief inspector, and he smelt trouble as soon as Carrozza brought it up.

They were sitting round the Head of the Art and Antiques Squad's desk. Carrozza, who was from the FBI, was on about Botticelli's portrait of Lorenzo delle Bandenere.

Five years ago Count Eugenio delle Bandenere, Monte Carlo, had sold it to Maxwell Silverman International, London. Silverman had sold it to Sampson Grenfell Korndorffer, Long Island, and when old Korndorffer died, it had come on the New York market.

Frank Short pricked up his ears at the name of Silverman. He had unfinished business with friend Max. "But that picture was right," he said. "Been in the Bandenere family since it was painted. Though the early provenance . . ."

Carrozza cut in. "Know something, Busby?" Busby was Detective Chief Superintendent Busby Papworth, Head of A & A, otherwise known as Ayatollah bloody Titworth, otherwise the Guv. "Know something? This guy's got it all in there."

It was true. The Korndorffer sale had been full of Florentine Renaissance, which was Frank Short's thing. He could have reeled off half the catalogue by heart.

"But was it so darn right?" Carrozza's face was mostly eyebrows. They shot up. "Now I have to tell you this, gentlemen.

The one and only art and antiques cop in New York takes a look at the Maxwell Silverman operation there. Now maybe it's on the level, but in the course of that look this guy kind of asks around about this little Botticelli. Okay, so an expert can be defined as a guy who doesn't agree with another expert, check?" The eyebrows sought confirmation. "But like Shorty says, it's this early what's-is. Just one letter from the artist, asking for his money, then nothing in four hundred years, till in 1870 a guy named Cunningham spots it in one of the Bandenere villas. . . ."

Frank Short was beginning to see what was coming, and why the FBI were using Chuck Carrozza rather than the post or the Telex. He was also beginning to scent trouble.

". . . And at the same time this Cunningham spots another picture no one knows about. . . ."

Frank Short couldn't resist showing off. "Piero di Cosimo; *Diana and Actaeon.* And both of them turn up at the London Silverman and Maxie flogs them to old Korndorffer."

"He knows, you know," said Titworth, who was a professional Yorkshireman.

"Check. And a year or two later they're back on the market. The Botticelli goes to the Louvre Museum, Paris, France, and the Piero di Cosimo to . . ."

Frank Short looked at his chief. "Do you remember where it went, sir?"

A little surprisingly, Papworth did.

"So I guess that makes it kind of sensitive, because seemingly this Piero di Cosimo's—what's the word? provenance—isn't that strong either. So seeing I was coming to Europe on this study tour, my chiefs asked me to drop in rather than put it through channels. Because if either one of those pictures is a phoney . . . Anyway they thought you might care to take a look at the London angle, and if you do happen to come up with anything . . ."

Papworth said, "Point taken. Anything more?"

"That's about it, I guess."

"Right. Thanks, Chuck; we'll have a look at it for you. Have a good . . ."

Frank Short wasn't listening. This could be serious. Not so much for himself, as for his father.

Frank Short's name had been Franco Corti till the first of April, just a month ago, which was hardly the ideal date. His father, Antonio Corti, was a picture restorer from Florence who had operated in Soho since World War II—cleaning, restoring, a bit of dealing, especially in Florentine Renaissance. His restorations could be far too creative, and he worked a lot for Maxwell Silverman. "Sensitive," Carrozza'd said. He could say that again.

That Yank was, in his own language, a pain in the ass. It was partly the ribbing, partly his attitude to being Italian.

"Well, what do you know! As one wop to another, *ciao*."

"They don't call us wops here. We're Eyeties. The ones as talk rough say raddies."

"But hell, you changed your name. Why did you do a thing like that? Listen, I'm Chuck Carrozza; what's wrong with that, for Christ's sake? I'm an East Side dago and proud of it. You ashamed of being a wop or something?" Stirring up all the heart-searching and hassle just when he thought he'd settled things. For a while he had been ashamed to be Frank Short.

But Carrozza hadn't been to Italy, which made him one up. "Mind you, Chuck, the art, the *dolce vita* and that, that's terrific. But then you come up against the rottenness. Bent coppers, petty vendettas, politics. It all comes back to politics. Or money. Or sometimes both. Yes, Chuck, it did make me ashamed. . . ."

And his children; they were getting as schizophrenic as he was, going off to school each morning like good Londoners, then back to the Soho-Eyetie claustrophobia of Beak Street. Three generations crammed together over the Trattoria Vaccarino, where his wife's parents, the old Vaccarinos, held doggedly Italian sway.

So last winter when his father gave him that money, he had bought this house in Acton and changed his name. And just as he was settling down to being Frank Short, learning to garden, paying off the mortgage, making himself have tea and eggs and bacon for breakfast and beer and a ploughman's for lunch, Carrozza had to come and stir up the mud.

But that wasn't dangerous. What was dangerous was the ribbing. It had started at last night's private view with the suit he was wearing. ". . . Don't tell me you got that on a British cop's salary. Who is this guy, Busby? What's he get paid, for Christ's sake?"

So he had explained about the advance legacy and being difficult to fit at five foot four with a forty-six-inch chest and thirty-six waist, so he'd gone overboard and ordered this suit from a top West End tailor.

"So your poppa in the art business gives you handouts? Hey, Busby, if an art and antiques cop starts taking handouts from some kind of a dealer or something, what does that make him? Maybe you want to investigate this guy."

He had a point, too, because when Frank Short had joined A & A, he and his father weren't speaking, and they'd stayed that way till last summer. But since then . . . Perhaps it was a bit irregular, but hell . . .

The private view where Carrozza ribbed him had been at the Silverman Gallery, Duke Street St. James's. Vee Bugler, whose show it was and whose portrait of Frank Short was in the window, had sent him half a dozen cards, and for the sake of seeing Max Silverman's face when a posse of detectives turned up, he had distributed them round A & A.

He got there about six and signed the book (and in the end it was debatable whether more of the general aggro and agony stemmed from that signature or from Carrozza, though the killer was *cherchez la femme*). By the time the others arrived, he had kissed Vee and talked to her father, Sir Frederick Bugler, in his wheelchair; he had taken note of Fiona the receptionist, whom he remembered because she had blue eyes and black hair and smelt good; he had drunk several glasses of champagne with Denise Verdier, who had kept house for Sir Fred till last summer, and who smelt exciting; and he had caught a flash of hate from Silverman's normally expressionless eyes. Whereupon friend Max strolled over, all smooth and affable, to join him and Denise. Last time they met, he had thrown Frank Short out of the gallery.

"Isn't she good, Inspector? Don't you think she's good?" Frank Short didn't think she was, he knew. "You mark my words; we're launching a major talent tonight. More champagne? Of course you will. Fiona my dear, champagne for the Inspector. And Inspector, a word in your ear before your father arrives. He tells me he has given you a painting."

Alarm bells rang in Frank Short's head. His father had indeed given him a painting. A little *Annunciation*, school of Fra Angelico, that could almost have been by the master himself. The old man called it a studio work and swore he'd done nothing to it that the National Gallery wouldn't.

Frank Short nodded to Silverman without speaking, and the big silken voice went on, "He showed it to me and I thought it was pretty, though I confess to major doubts about its authenticity. In fact, I made him an offer, but we could not agree terms. I don't think he really wanted to sell. So I just wished to beg you, should you ever be interested in disposing of it, please not to forget us here. . . ."

A landed-gentry-ish joke had been going round the Embassy in Rome—about the three most dangerous things: a quiet bull, an empty gun, a friendly Russian. What price friend Max as the Russian?

"How much?" Frank asked. Not that he would have dreamt of selling.

"Ah! You are too quick for me. I had not yet reached a figure. Let me see—your father turned down ten thousand. Fifteen, shall we say?"

What kind of a mug did he take him for? Papà was bound to

turn that down, though he'd only given two grand himself. (". . . and the lady was overjoyed, Franco, overjoyed!")

"No, thanks, Mr. Silverman. I can't say as I'm really keen on selling. But if I change my mind, I won't forget you." He wouldn't forget him regardless.

Denise smiled with unexpected malice. "Oh, Frank! You must demand at least five times what he asks. Ten would be better, or even twenty."

He caught her eye and something happened.

It was the first time he had thought of her like that. As a prospect. Denise was tiny. She wore four-inch heels, but he could still see over her head. She was dressed in glossy, loose, heavily tapered slacks and an ethnic top, and in that light, with her straight blond hair, she looked like a child. When Silverman drifted away, there was a smile on Frank Short's face (a great rarity), and a message on hers: Come and get me.

Franco Corti would never have ducked a challenge like that, and he hoped Frank Short wouldn't. He asked, "And what are you doing with yourself, now that . . . ?" He hadn't seen her for three months.

Her shrug, like all her movements, was a work of art. "I live. A bit of this, a bit of that. It is not interesting. But tell me about yourself. You have bought your house?"

"Been in for a fortnight." What if she was knocking on forty? None the worse for that. Before long, his arm was round her waist.

A tap on his shoulder, an ambiance out of harmony with the champagne, a creaky male voice. "Franco!"

He turned, and Denise with him, feather-light, clasping his great hand to her side. *"Papà! Come stai?"* The old man had spent almost forty years in England but never done much about the language; they had always talked Italian.

"Not so bad, Franco, not so bad. Was that the famous portrait? *Dio mio!*" (For him, painting had ended with Leonardo.) He woke up to Denise's presence and switched to his laboured English. "Good evening, madam. Antonio Corti."

"Denise Verdier." They shook hands, continental style. Old Corti was no taller than Frank Short but narrower in the shoulders, and recognizably his father. He had done his best to look smart, but nature was against him with his paunch and his bulging nose. And not only nature: granny-specs, a crew cut, a baggy grey suit over a cardigan, and no tie. A visibly womanless man, he had been a widower for thirty-four years. Frank Short squeezed Denise's waist and decided he was making up for woman-deprivation in boyhood.

And here was Max Silverman like a great purring cat, with a drink for old Antonio. "A great man, your father, an exquisite workman; you've no idea how good. And a very perceptive collector. One day, Antonio, you must let me tell you what those pictures are worth and you'll get a surprise. Your father's a rich man, Inspector, though he's too modest to let us see it."

Well, he'd settled money on the kids, but nothing on Frank Short till last year, and then only seventeen thousand. Before that they'd hardly been on speaking terms. Old Corti hadn't fancied a son in the police.

Only seventeen thousand? What about the little *Annunciation* then, workshop of Fra Angelico? Workshop? Or . . . ? It can't! Things like that don't happen. A genuine Fra Angelico? It'd be worth millions. But look at friend Max, into his friendly-Russian act. Got a whiff of something, hasn't he, and what else? He and his nice clean record. Max Silverman's record was so clean that in 1948, when he was nicked for receiving, he had won a farthing's damages for wrongful arrest.

Frank Short watched him talking to old Antonio, his eyes dissociated from the mobile face. ". . . You remember the little Boucher?" (Boucher? Antonio Corti.) "It's gone. To a very good friend; not quite at list price, but one has to look after one's . . ."

Max Silverman stopped in his tracks. Frank Short could never figure out how he knew, but when his eyes followed Silverman's towards the door, there was the Guv, looking like a Guards sergeant-major trying to look like a Guards officer, with Carrozza the visiting fireman in a pink checked shirt and mauve tie, and queuing behind them to sign the book the two sergeants, Keith and Jackie Billings, back from their honeymoon.

The second they moved, Max Silverman edged past him, looking serious, to inspect the book. Frank Short gave him time to study it, then introduced him to Papworth.

Friend Max never batted an eyelid, but it was a laugh. Frank Short knew how he felt about policemen. So did the Guv. Frank Short watched them stalking each other with broad smiles and bristling hackles. Before long the Guv was instructing Silverman about modern art in his roughest Yorkshire: ". . . conning the public, egged on by a load of boys as ought to know better. They can't bloody draw, they can't bloody paint, so they get hold of some crafty gimmick gets written up as the last stroke of bloody genius. . . ."

He left them to it, thinking of his portrait in the window. That was modern enough. By Hockney out of Bacon, would you say? No, you wouldn't. It was by Vee.

It was a remarkable painting of a remarkable subject. People made phrases about Frank Short: "Out of a Florentine battle-piece," "The Centurion," "The Roman Emperor." Dark, melting eyes in a warrior's face, the gravity, the granite, the wide, thin mouth, the flattened, arrogant nose. And the scar, eight months old, slicing the wing of his right nostril and his upper lip. He was childishly proud of his scar.

Vee had understood that. What a good painter. Look at the little Arezzo landscape. Only three fifty? A souvenir? An investment? A sense of power came over him. He could afford it. He pushed through the crowd. "Excuse me, miss. Number eight—I'd like to buy it."

"Hear that, Busby? He bought one! Shorty just bought one. Three hundred fifty pounds. Three hundred fifty on a little picture like that. That guy's really loaded." Damn that Carrozza, barking like a bleeding guard-dog. He'll have bloody Titworth barking next.

That time when a brick, a note about co-operation, and two hundred pounds came through the Trattoria Vaccarino's window for him, you could just see the old devil thinking what could have happened if that PC hadn't been there. No one trusted anyone these days, with Countryman still fresh and CIB2 and coppers resigning sudden-like without explanation or being shunted into the sticks. . . .

But Papworth just grinned and said, "Oh aye?" Well, he would, wouldn't he? And . . . *Gesù Maria!* Look at that!

There, in front of his eyes, was his father leaving the gallery with Denise on his arm. And he remembered that great sleek Silverman voice, and it had been in front of her, "Your father's a rich man, Inspector."

The she-Frog. The bitch.

CHAPTER 2

ABOVE SUSPICION

"Shorty?" It was twenty-four hours later.

"Yes, Guv?"

"That lass's picture of you. If it's not too personal a question, how much was it?"

"Nothing, Guv; it was a Christmas present."

"Oh aye?"

Now why did he want to know that? A nosy bastard or he wouldn't have got where he was, but not one for idle curiosity. Titworth's curiosity was never idle.

"Look, Shorty, I don't want you to take this personally, but you've not done so bad with presents these last few months. First you'd your dad's money, then this portrait, and if Silverman's prices are anything to go by, it could have cost four figures to commission that. Now we know you here, Shorty. I'd say you're above suspicion. But there's some as wouldn't, and it's their business nosing round the stack to sniff out the wrong 'uns. . . ."

Sod that Carrozza. I knew he'd get Titworth barking. And what am I expected to do? Give it all back or something? That really would look suspicious.

None of this added to his peace of mind while he eased himself into the life-style of Frank Short, apprentice commuter, apprentice gardener, apprentice handyman, as inept about the house as young Franco had been in his father's workshop. He hadn't known how traumatic the change would be.

At the Yard it mattered less; he was still Shorty. And it was good when on promotion he moved out of the general office into a glorified kennel shared with Bob Wellow. Old Bob was the only other chief inspector, and with Detective Superintendent Hunt, Deputy Head, they constituted the Guv's general staff.

Hunt was on a senior command course at Bramshill; old Bob was up to his neck in a tricky and complex bugging case (for some reason A & A looked after industrial espionage); the Guv, deprived of his deputy, was having to cope himself with an epidemic of stolen paintings; so the Carrozza File, as Keith Billings called it, was on Frank Short's plate.

Mercifully, because if it *was* Antonio Corti, he'd be the first to know, and perhaps the old man could take a trip to somewhere with no extradition treaty. And Frank Short, foiled of his prey, would be that furious. . . . But with his father as a suspect he could never stay on the case. So if the old man did have to take off, he'd better not be a suspect till he'd gone, and even that could be dicey for Frank Short.

Where did you begin then? The Botticelli was in Paris, so you'd have to get the Frogs on to it, but the Piero di Cosimo was in London, and the obvious thing was to have it vetted, and by the best in the business. The big auction houses weren't right for this, and it was hardly the National Gallery's job. He decided on the Gruenwald Foundation.

It was all very discreet; the Guv, who could be diplomatic when he set his mind to it, made the first approach to the royal residence, and Frank Short found himself inspecting the painting in company with a discreet and charming mandarin who knew just about everything about pictures and took it all rather lightly as long as you didn't.

There was nothing wrong on the surface. Style, brushwork, technique, subject, composition, colour. Probably early, experi-

mental oil-paint; an unobtrusive surface craquelure, traces of old
gallery varnish overlaid with mastic—nothing wrong there. Out
of the frame, the panel looked okay too; probably poplar, which
was normal, certainly old; in good nick except for a few long-
abandoned beetle-holes.

"Can you see anything wrong with it?" asked the mandarin.

Frank Short shook his head. "No. Can't say as I can. That's a
nice little painting, that is, even if it does turn out to be dodgy."

"It is indeed, which is why the purchase was authorized. It
would be sad if it were faulted. Still, we can't impede the wheels
of justice; that would never do."

It was indeed a nice little painting, in the artist's pastoral-
mythological vein. Mountains, a glade, a glimpse of distant water.
Horsemen, dogs. Diana with her bow and arrows, Actaeon grow-
ing antlers. Wild beasts, nymphs, centaurs peeping from behind
the trees. In fact, a typical Piero di Cosimo. Though, "D'you
know, sir, there is just one little niggle. . . ."

"Oh?"

"It's the spirit of the thing. I mean usually he's all sort of mys-
terious—you know—romantic and that; sad, if you like. But this
. . . well, there isn't any sadness; it looks almost like he's stuck
the mystery on afterwards, see what I mean? These creatures
among the trees . . ."

"An element of inconsistency? Surely not an invalidating one?
But seeds of doubt all the same. What a pity, *what* a pity. Ah,
well. You have my notes on its history? Good. I think that's everything. I won't wish you good luck unless the absence of crime
counts as such, but simply a very good morning. Be kind to it,
Chief Inspector, won't you?"

Next stop the Gruenwald, and a chance to show them his little
Annunciation as well. Not that they would put it through the
labs for him, but they might still spot something.

The Gruenwald escorted the royal purchase to the labs with
due reverence, then, with not too much reluctance, looked at the

Annunciation, and the reluctance vanished. "I *say!* My goodness, Chief Inspector, you've got something there. Now that really is interesting. I say, Miranda, do come and look at this. . . ." However, tests would be useful only for dating because the master's assistants would use his own materials and techniques. "But we'll give it a quick whirl. Cost? Oh, I think we can lose that in the bushes."

That was nice of them. Frank Short went back to the Yard to tackle the Sûreté.

How discreet did he have to be? Did he need to drag in the Piero di Cosimo? Why not just ask about the Botticelli? Usual channels, through Interpol. He sat down to draft a message.

. . . *Our interest in this case centres round the role of Maxwell Silverman International.* . . . He grunted. He hadn't said where his own interest centred, his interest and the worry that gnawed, day in, day out, like a worm in his gut. The role of Antonio Corti.

A fortnight passed, and May, which had come in grey and cold, turned shirt-sleeve warm. Paper washed incessantly over his desk, forcing him to be chair-borne, which he hated. He was settling into Balfour Road too; so, to his relief, was Teresa, though it could have been just her work load. Teresa throve on hard graft. When she gave up the Trattoria's books, she had been bored and restless. At present there was plenty to keep her busy; the difficult times for her lay ahead, because once she'd got things organized, she'd have finished work by ten and the fun would begin.

The children were at Beak Street with their grandparents till the end of term, so Frank Short could dig and spray and plant to his heart's content—the garden had been an overgrown scrap-heap when they moved in—telling himself this stage was bound to be boring, and bound to be puzzling because he hardly knew a rose-bush from a carrot. It was frustrating as well. You stuck in these seeds and that, like the book said, and all you got was weeds.

The phone was in, thanks to the Guv, who had put the fear of God and all his Yorkshiremen into British Telecom, and a fortnight after Frank's visit to the Gruenwald, there was a call from the woman called Miranda.

"Mr. Short? Oh, good. I'm ringing to let you know we've finished with your *Annunciation,* so any time you care to collect . . ."

"Thanks. I'll be along. What's the verdict?"

"A-one, absolutely A-one, as far as we can tell. You knew it had been very recently cleaned?"

"That's right."

"I don't know who the restorer was, but he did it quite admirably; *most* sensitive cleaning, the absolute minimum of repainting, and in tempera, which is so unusual among commercial restorers. I do congratulate you on your choice. You couldn't tell me who it was, could you?"

"A man called Corti. Works in London but learnt his trade in Florence. . . ."

"Corti? Do I know the name? I shall certainly remember it. Do please congratulate him if you're in touch. . . ."

"I will, miss. And you say the picture's okay?"

"As far as can be judged from our tests. You do understand, of course, that they could not be comprehensive, or even thorough, so our opinion is in no way conclusive. As you doubtless know, this is one of the few areas where a negative is easier to prove than a positive."

"We get that sort in police work too, miss. And as between a studio work and . . . ?"

"Fra Angelico himself? Impossible to say. We certainly cannot rule him out on technical or indeed aesthetic grounds. I think if I were you, I'd get a really tip-top critical opinion."

"Which means in your book?"

"Oh, Willison, don't you think? Would you like a letter of introduction? And do let us know what he says; we're all so interested."

"Thanks, miss; I'd appreciate that. And the other one, the Piero di Cosimo?" (Piero di Cosimo? Antonio Corti? Please, God, don't let it be Papà. . . .)

"Yes. Well . . . well . . . let me be honest, Mr. Short. There *are* one or two small points. But it's early days; a good deal still needs doing before we can give a considered opinion, and in the circumstances to give an unconsidered one would be a trifle rash, don't you think?"

Gervase Willison, professor of fine art at one of the trendier universities, sat down beside Frank Short on a settee made seemingly of outsize Mars bars. He was a pundit of the younger sort, a popularizer, good value in a quiz show, a trustee of the Tate, and a major authority on the quattrocento "A picture to show me? But how nice! Well, Mr. Short?"

He unwrapped the *Annunciation* and handed it to the professor, who took it to the light and held it out at arm's length for a long, concentrated scrutiny, with his fashionably cropped head on one side. "Yes. Oh, yes. Oh, but that's *charming*. Don't you think that's pwetty?"

He did.

"Wenaissance, of course, and Flowentine in the manner of Fwa Angelico, and Miwanda says genuine, and I'm sure she's wight." Those *r*'s weren't just put on for the box. He'd thought they were.

"One can counterfeit the parts, the dwawing, colour, iconogwaphy; one can use the pwoper materials, the wight techniques, but one can't imitate the whole. If you wemember Van Meegewen—a *pwince* of forgery—it was Malwaux who pointed out that his Chwist that everyone had taken for a Vermeer for *ages* had a face like a film star. No film stars in Vermeer's day, Mr. Short.

No, if this were not contempowawy work, one would see it, though one couldn't perhaps pin it down. But it would be there, the elusive taint to the fwagwance, the burgundy cut with Algerian, though not burgundy, not this time. A claret, perhaps? Why, champagne! Surely the Italian Wenaissance is the champagne of art?"

Frank Short said he hadn't really thought about it.

"Yes, I think we can take that as established, a pwedella panel of the Flowentine spwingtime. But who did it? Aye, there's the wub—who did it? The heart would like to say the blessed Angelico himself, but the poor thing must be wuled by the head. So let's look for areas of doubt, shall we? . . ."

He took it apart inch by inch, brushstroke by brushstroke—the line, the still naive perspective, the gorgeous cinnabar red of the angel's robe, the tooled gold, the lapis-lazuli blue; the underpainting in the Gruenwald's X-rays, as crisp and sure as the surface. He got out his magnifying glass and half a library of coloured photographs, and he couldn't fault it. An hour later he was immersed, speaking as if Frank Short weren't there.

"A discovewy, I do declare. A weal miwaculous discovewy." He looked up with an expression of rapture, and for one terrifying moment Frank Short thought he would embrace him, but instead he grasped his hand. "Oh, *congwatulations*, Mr. Short. I'm delighted for you, so tewwibly delighted!" There was something so innocent about him. "May I call you Fwank? I'm Gervase. Now tell me all about it. Where did it come from?"

Frank Short told him how his father had bought it from this lady in a cottage in Norfolk, and found himself explaining his own origins.

". . . A Flowentine? But how lovely! How doubly lucky you are, Fwank. You're a cwaftsman yourself, no doubt?"

"No such luck. As a matter of fact, I'm a policeman."

If he had said he was a murderer, dope-smuggler, and child-rapist, Gervase Willison could not have responded more dramatically. "That's not *cwicket*, Fwank! You should have said! If you're in the police, you should *tell* people. How do I know you're not here to spy on me, though God knows I've nothing to hide? As if that meant anything to people like you. If one's pwogwessive, if one's gay, one gets hawassed. Twumped-up charges, fabwicated evidence—what were you going to plant, Fwank?"

"Calm down, Professor, please. I'm here as a private individual; and if I wasn't, I'm from the Art Squad, not Special Branch. I don't give a damn about your politics or your private life; I came for your expert opinion, and I'm grateful for it. Do you think I'd have said who I was if I was spying on you? 'Course I wouldn't.'"

Willison actually sniffed and wiped an eye, and Frank Short half-registered something odd.

"Oh, all wight. Sowwy. I'm *so* highly stwung. It was the *surpwise*, you see, such a shock—it put me quite off balance. Forgive me, Fwank, do please forgive me. Because if you haven't shown me a weal, *yummy* Fwa Angelico this afternoon, you can awwest me for a fwaud. Pwomise! No, I go too far. One can never be weally sure; you do understand that?"

But it could hardly have been coincidence that in a day or two headlines started popping up where you would expect:

PIG IN GILDED STY *How come, Mister Short?*

COPPER STRIKES GOLD

POLICE MILLIONAIRE SCANDAL *Against a background of mounting police corruption we reveal . . .*

And pretty soon the headlines popped up somewhere else that you'd expect. On Papworth's desk.

CHAPTER 3

GIGGLES

. . . Honest, Mr. Papworth, I never dreamt it was in that league, and nor did the old guv'nor, and he reckons he's an optimist. I mean a genuine Fra Angelico, it's ridiculous. What's a copper going to do with a thing like that?"

"You're forced to do something; you can't just stick it up in the carzey and forget it. You've to protect your property; security, insurance—aye, and temperature and humidity, you've to think of that. . . ."

"I dunno, sir. I just don't know. I mean the insurance for a start, it's three quid a year per thousand. That's three thousand nicker on a million. It's just not on."

"Then stop mucking about, lad. Put the bugger in the bank and have done with it. Or flog it and retire."

He'd worked it out a dozen times; if it fetched a million, there'd be 10 per cent commission, plus VAT, which came to a hundred and fifteen grand; then capital-gains tax on the rest, less the two thousand his father had given for it. That would leave him with £620,100 in his pocket—less than two thirds. Did it really cost £380,000 to cash a million? And that Silverman had the chutzpah to offer £15,000.

The trouble was it was so sodding beautiful it hurt, and knowing it was right made it more so. How could he part with it? ". . . I dunno, Guv. I just don't know."

"You said that before. Come on, lad, square up to the bowling. That's your problem, Shorty, and I wish I'd one like it. It'll not go away, you know. But as for this lot"—the headlines and the stories under them—"that's the Force's problem, not just yours. Is that understood?"

"Yes, sir."

"You know what they'll be saying? No smoke without flame. It'll be hard for some not to think there's something to it. But I'll speak as I find. I've sized you up, lad. You're no bent copper. Just so it stays that way, right?"

Just so it stays that way! Oh, Shorty, how we trust you! We love you, baby, we worship the ground you tread on, kiss your arse and tell you you're beautiful. The finesse of a bull elephant with a hangover. "Right, sir. This lot then, it's the Force's problem. That's great. But it's me's getting libelled. Would you be kind enough to tell me, Mr. Papworth, sir, what the Force proposes to do about it?"

"Bugger-all, like as not. They're crafty, these lads; you'll not get 'em for libel in a hurry unless they're looking to go to law. And if we go issuing denials, they'll only twist 'em so folks think we've something to deny."

"Can't we lean on them a bit?"

"Police harassment? Just what they want, don't they, so's they can make a bloody great song and dance about it. No, lad, you've to grin and bear it. And that's that; there's work to be done. Back on the beat."

"Franco!" Antonio Corti on his doorstep in slippers and cardy in a temperature worthy of July, coughing and spitting out his cigarette stub before embracing him. "Come in. Shut the door. You should be careful about coming here, Franco; there are people who could misinterpret your presence, and they are not *simpatici*."

"*Naturalmente.* So I came by taxi. You are not being watched; it is only chance observations we need to guard against."

"*Capito.* You are thoughtful and I appreciate your thought. A good son, yes, even if you are a policeman. Come on up."

It was hot in here! And it could do with an air-freshener. When did he last have a window open? Or dust or empty an ashtray or sweep the lino? Lino, for pity's sake, and in two-tone yuk-brown, and this in the eighties. It was here when we moved in, me and poor Mamma, thirty-four years ago. Lino, gilt Venetian chairs, gorgeous but falling apart same as Venice; a little rolltop desk that belonged to Scrooge, and curtains in the fat-moth business. Grappa's okay, though, a very nice grappa. Not Frank Short's drink, but when in Soho, do like the raddies do, and anyway it's all he has—that and Uncle Paolo's vino. And his grandchildren and his work and his pictures. A rich man? Why not? Look at those pictures. Can't see the wallpaper for them, and they're not all home-made. Doesn't do it from the bottom up, though; he likes something to build on. . . .

Meanwhile, making chit-chat, sidestepping disapproval of Frank Short and Acton, remembering the private view. "Very nice. I hope you enjoyed it, Papà."

"I did; indeed I did. I like your friends. I did not know you had such sympathetic friends."

Uh-huh! "Anyone in particular?"

"Ah! Oho!" (Giggle, giggle.) "One charming elegant lady, very gracious; very kind to an old workman . . ."

"Madame Verdier? You know she was Sir Frederick Bugler's mistress?" If that wasn't true, it was her bad luck. Cow.

"Was she now? Then Sir Frederick was very fortunate. A lady like that would not stay long unprotected; he did well to win her."

"Oh he did, did he?"

"Indeed he did. And she is a magnificent cook as well."

"As well as *what*, Papà?"

"As her kindness, vivacity, charm. I tell you, Franco, the man who lands that little fish is to be much envied."

What's she been up to with him? Wrapping him round her little finger. Playing easy to get? How easy? How far have they gone? He's like a cat with a gallon of cream. And he's only sixty-four. Dammit, he could be perfectly capable . . . But hell, a fastidious bint like her? Fastidious? No accounting for taste, is there? Look at Jackie Nunn: dried-up old stick, then along comes Keithy-boy and . . .

Forget her. You're well out of that. What'll she do? Con a couple of pictures out of the old feller and bye-bye Denise? Like in that Piero di Cosimo: a shy, elusive creature of the forest. All you'll see'll be her pretty little arse bobbing off into the woods. "Papà?"

A cough or two, a little metallic in timbre. "Yes?"

"That little *Annunciation* you gave me, God bless you. Have you seen the papers?"

"What papers?"

"The subversive ones, the anti-everything, satirical rags, lefty propaganda sheets."

"Why should I read such trash?"

"Then you do not know. They have got hold of the story that you gave it to me, the little picture."

"And why should I not give my son a picture? Of what interest to them is that?"

"I must explain. I had business at the Gruenwald, so I took it along. It is always interesting to have an opinion from such people." The old man nodded gravely and lowered his head to peer over the granny-specs. "They made a few tests. They were full of praise for the way you had cleaned it. I gave them your name; I hope you do not mind."

A beaming "No indeed!"

"And finally they say it is a genuine studio work, as we suspected, and quite possibly by the master himself."

Silence, but a new depth in the eyes quizzing over the spectacles.

"They sent me to Gervase Willison, and do you know what he says? That picture's no studio work but a genuine Fra Angelico."

A long, long silence; then the one word, "Good."

"But you see, Papà, that's what the press have got hold of. A dealer called Corti gives a policeman called Short a picture worth who knows what? Millions. No word that you are my father. So it looks bad, *capisci?*"

"Yes, Franco, I see. But surely the relationship can be explained. . . ."

"Oh, yes; that's not really the problem. But it's still bad for me. . . ."

"You know what, Franco? It's bad for you, okay. But what about me? I tell you, I have dealings with people who do not like their associates to be friendly with policemen. And this is in the newspapers! I don't think I like this. *Gesù Maria!* I don't think I like this at all."

"Papà?" (It was a third of a bottle of grappa later.) "Papà—this Fra Angelico. Nothing the National Gallery wouldn't have done? Is that true?"

"Of course." No histrionics, no protestations or invoking of saints; not the usual violin solo ("I never deceive, Franchino; trust is everything. If a man I trust tells me some *patacca*"—some faked-up piece of grot—"is genuine, who am I, a poor simple workman, to question his word? Especially if the money's right." Boo-hoo, sniff sniff.) None of that, just a quiet, even dignified *of course.* I have to believe the old villain. Dammit, I do believe him.

"The Gruenwald and Professor Willison and my father in perfect harmony?" (Definition of an expert: a guy who disagrees with another expert?) "Papà, I'm so delighted, so *grateful.*"

"Delighted? Grateful? And you repay your old father with fear.

It frightens me, Franco, to think how some people will interpret this."

Frank Short looked at the moist brown eyes behind their lenses, the grey stubbled head, the grey features that mirrored his own except for the nose, and shared their apprehension.

"Which people, Papà? Tell me. Then perhaps we could do something to help . . ."

"Who? The police? Help from the police? What are you saying?" The reflexes of a lifetime.

"All right; if that's the way you want it. I was only trying to help."

"I know. You're a good son and I thank you, but . . ."

"Leave it, Papà. Listen, there's something I wanted to ask you. You remember the Korndorffer sale in New York? . . ." He passed on Carrozza's account of the two pictures from the Bandenere collection that Silverman had sold to old Korndorffer: the Botticelli or similar in the Louvre, the Piero di Cosimo or similar still at the Gruenwald. . . . "So clearly there are grounds for suspicion, and as I know you do some work for Silverman, I wondered . . . Is there anything you can tell me, Papà? Anything you would *like* to tell me? In confidence, if you wish. You see . . . Well, let's put it this way: It could help me to assess the degree of importance—of effort, *capisci?*—I should give to the investigation. . . ." What are you saying, man? That's not Frank Short talking, that's no straight-batted Englishman, that's a bleeding Eyetie. It's hardly even Franco Corti, because whatever else he was, he wasn't bent; he just had the sense to stay clear of situations like this, and if that meant keeping out of his father's life for twenty years, whose fault was that?

"I think, Franco, I can tell you as much as I know, which is very little. I remember Maxie getting those pictures; he was very pleased, but they were both in good condition and he had no need of my services. I don't think I even saw them."

He looked as if he was telling the truth. But he would, wouldn't he? He'd hardly go around with a placard saying "Liar."

"Okay. Now assume for a moment those pictures aren't right; they're a pair of bleeding *patacche*. You haven't been near them. But someone has; someone's got at them or painted them from scratch or something. Who, Papà? Any idea at all?"

"No, son. No. As it happens, I have no information. And if I had . . . This is not something you should ask of me, Franco. You know my position. I am trusted and I do not betray trust, not even to my son, and certainly not to the police. And when this revoltingness in the newspapers becomes known, as it is bound to, then that trust will be weakened, very gravely weakened." He was flushed and his voice was rising, with an unfamiliar brassy note in it. "Dangerously weakened, Franco, and I would be mad a million times over were I to endanger it further by *denunziare a quei coglioni disgraziati*. Understood? Now please do not refer to the subject again."

Denunziare and that meant roughly "grassing to bloody filth."

"Papà, forgive me. I am sorry. It was thoughtless of me to mention it, but when a man is under strain . . . All right, Papà, let's forget it. Except that if you ever do change your mind and wish for protection, your son is at your disposal with all the resources of Scotland Yard. . . ."

A grave, silent nod, and after a pause, "All right, Franco. It is stupid that we should quarrel. A final glass?"

"No, thank you, Papà. I must think of my health. And look at the time! Can I ring for a cab? Teresa will think I am with a woman or something!"

"Perhaps you should be, son. A change sometimes does a man good." (Giggle, giggle, giggle; cough, cough, cough.) "Oh, and Franco—"

"Yes?"

"That was a very fine suit you had on at the private view. Madame Verdier admired it very much, and she keeps on at me—

you know women, Franco, always on at a man; one can resist for so long, but . . . Look, you wouldn't do me the favour of giving me your tailor's name?"

"Why, of course, Papà." (And my brand of soap, too, you old scoundrel?)

"Short speaking." "Short" by itself sounded odd.

"Frank! This is Denise. Frank, I've been meaning to ring for ages. You are well?"

"Not very. Why?" (She-Frog. Bitch.) Thank heaven it wasn't Teresa who picked up the phone.

"Oh, I'm *sorry!* It's nothing serious, is it?"

Why waste effort on politeness? "Pissed off, that's all."

There was that long, expressive, deep-throated, flared-lipped, stage-whispered French hybrid of *oh* and *ah*—"*Oaoaoah!* But that's no *good,* Frank! I must cheer you up."

"By chatting me up and going off with someone else? Great."

"*Oaoah! Mais non!* It was you who went off and left me with your father!"

"But I—"

"Yes, you did; you were with me and Max and Antonio, and your friends came and you joined them and left us alone."

His friends? Titworth, Carrozza, the Billingses? "Good grief, I suppose I did. But—"

"Your father was very good to me. You're so *lucky,* Frank; he's such a sweet little man, and I hope you appreciate it."

"But—"

"*Oaoah,* come on, Frank. I did not ring to talk about your father but about you. Frank, I would so much like to see your collection. Do you think it would be possible?"

Collection, for pity's sake! One mini-blockbuster of a Fra Angelico, a blow-up of the Gibbonsian Tondo in black and white, a dozen picture postcards of Florence, and two Vee Buglers she'd seen already. Some collection.

"There's nothing to see, only what was at the Silverman. Well, only one thing."

"But what a thing, Frank! Antonio told me about it. I can't wait to see it, honestly. *Please*, Frank . . ."

That *please* had star quality. He hadn't a chance. "All right, then. Look, I'll ring back, only . . ."

"Your wife? She is around? Why, of *course*, Frank. My number is . . ."

He rang from a call-box an hour later and they fixed an evening when Teresa would be busy at the Trattoria. He put the phone down feeling mixed up. Overjoyed, guilty, scared. Of being caught out, of the woman's power over him, of his own paralysis. Father round one little finger, son round the other. Humiliating. But what little fingers.

CHAPTER 4

FINGERS

He found out all about Denise's fingers when she came to see him. It was strange with this scrap of a thing not half his weight —they stood on the scales in turn, naked, and she was seven stone one to his fourteen six—strange and a little off-putting, and he had to forget Frank Short and revert to being Franco Corti, and then she was quite an experience.

But somehow incomplete, as if technique, not nature, was at work. Physically it was great. Humanly it seemed to demote them both. That sort of carry-on usually left him a little guilty, a little defiant, but thoroughly smug. But this . . . He felt ashamed.

And frightened, in case Teresa spotted something when she got back. But she didn't. She arrived dog-tired about eleven and went straight to bed.

That was the way she liked it. If Teresa wasn't clapped out at the end of the day, she'd get neurotic and couldn't sleep till she'd spent half the night nagging away her neurosis, and in the morning he'd be like a wet dishcloth and she couldn't think why. Unless he could get her turned on and relax her by other means, but that was difficult and unpredictable and needed luck. Franco Corti's, not Frank Short's.

Teresa, like Denise but less so, was the small wiry sort, though her thighs were spreading. She was dark-skinned, neat, and quietly-dressed, and had been pretty as a girl. Not that she was bad-looking now, but the fire had gone. Or rather, it was reserved for work.

The move had been traumatic for her. She had threatened divorce over the change from Corti to Short and about the children's first names. She had put her foot down and they had stayed Gino, Sylvia, Cesare, Graziella, and Antonio. At Balfour Road she plunged furiously into home-making. Frank Short, who was no workman, found himself banished to the garden. And now, with Balfour Road almost finished, she was spending half her time at the Trattoria. He supposed they were still married.

He slept well that night, and was up at six for his exercises and bath and bacon and eggs. He took Teresa her coffee in good time for the battle of the tube and a walk from Hyde Park Corner to the Yard that made him feel really chipper. The park on a fine May morning, the savour of Denise and the thought of more to come, of all the free evenings before the school holidays made him forget the guilts and worries. Ten whole weeks for pleasure; a short hot summer of love.

His in-tray was overflowing. Case reports, circulars, references from other departments, internal memos. He waded in and by the time the girl brought the external post, it was nine tenths cleared. He set the rest aside to run through the outside stuff.

Ah. Now this was interesting. It was the Gruenwald report on the Piero di Cosimo, and none of your quick whirls but the full treatment. Or as full as was possible, because as they pointed out —though they didn't need to for Frank Short—to examine a picture fully you have to clean it. All the technology in the world won't tell you what's there till you've stripped off the varnish and the repaints and can see for yourself. And that was out of the question.

But here were the X-rays and infra-reds and enlargements and raking-light shots, with detailed write-ups that amounted to this: panel, okay; gesso, okay; drawing (infra-reds), okay; underpainting—what you could see in the X-rays—okay. Paint probably tempera with oil glazes, which was what you'd expect, and the whole thing "characteristic of Piero di Cosimo."

The condition was good. Paint-film excellent, adhesion excellent, cracking minimal and apparently natural. As on the Fra Angelico, some blackened old gallery varnish had been cleaned off and replaced within the last twenty years by mastic. There were traces of overpainting having been removed, and what damage there was, and there was unusually little, had been restored with exceptional skill, almost certainly in tempera.

. . . which is the second case we have seen recently of a private restorer using tempera. Repaints in oil tend to darken faster than the older, more stable colour. For this reason most major public galleries use tempera. However, tempera changes colour slightly on drying and again on varnishing, and so requires a great deal of time and skill for accurate matching; consequently it is rarely if ever used by commercial restorers.

They were a fraction narked that they hadn't been allowed to take paint-film samples for cross-sectional photomicrographs, which show individual grains of pigment. The shapes and sizes and colours of those grains say a lot about the origin of a picture, and are about the one thing no forger can reproduce.

Finally they pronounced that if the picture was a fake, it was brilliant and very elaborate, because not only had the Florentine methods been followed in detail, but things like damage, repairs, and traces of darkened varnish had been added too.

. . . Technically, we are unable to fault it, but we cannot but confess to a purely subjective uneasiness. Is its condition too good to be true? we ask ourselves, and we fear the answer may be yes. Photomicrographs could perhaps set our minds at rest, but as permission for sampling has been refused, doubtless for the best of reasons, we regret we must return an open verdict.

Frank Short mopped his forehead and clenched his eyes shut, feeling his whole face pucker, and murmured, "Tempera! Bloody hell!" Because he did know a private restorer who used the stuff. Antonio Corti.

"Shorty? Did you say something?" Bob Wellow looked up through eyes that drooped at the corners as if they could see half-way through a brick.

"Sorry. Talking to myself. Bad sign."

"Trouble, is it?" The voice had a Wessex roundness very suit-able to the kindly-uncle persona.

"Yes . . . well . . . sort of. You could call it that."

"Anything I can do?"

"Not really. Thanks."

"Right you are. I hope you didn't think I was prying or any-thing." Bob's reputation as an interrogator rested largely on his skill at not prying. Frank Short shut his mouth tight.

Old Bob could have been starting up some yarn of Hampshire cricket. "My old dad had a do a bit like yours, you know, and had to be careful of his ticker. The doc said we were to watch out for him sort of rubbing his left hand like it wasn't comfortable. His left little finger, the palm of the hand, or up the forearm . . ."

Frank Short dropped his left little finger like a hot chestnut. Hadn't noticed he was doing it. But there was something. As if his collarbone were catching a nerve now it was mended, or his shirt were tight under the arms.

"Trouble, eh? I reckon learning to live with your troubles is learning to live. You know what they say, Shorty? A trouble shared is trouble halved."

You had to say something, or he'd know you'd something to hide.

"It's the newspaper talk, Bob. All right, so I've got problems about the picture: insurance, security, and that, but it's the smears that hurt. Even the Guv . . . Doesn't believe a word, does he? 'Eeh, ba goom, I've sized yer oop and happen yer not bloody bent after all. Purer than t'driven bloody snow, you are. Joost so it stays that way.' Just so it stays that way. Bloody Titworth! He really makes it easy for you."

Old Bob reckoned the Guv had problems of his own. Had Shorty seen that wife of his? Haw, haw, haw! If you hadn't seen Ma Papworth, you hadn't seen life. "That little finger still bothering you?"

This time he went on massaging it. "That? It's this shirt. See how it catches? They all do. I'm always getting pins and needles." Which was not much more than the truth.

He didn't say he was always feeling guilty too. About some woman or other. About Teresa. About his mother from Naples, who'd died for him when he was only six. Worn herself to pieces coping in wartime Florence, with Papà a prisoner in the UK. His father had never seen him till she brought him to London. About bringing the kids up as Eyeties, about uprooting them and taking them to Acton. Or about going against Papà's wishes to become a copper. Or being Franco Corti or Frank Short, or eating too much or not going to mass . . .

And now Papà. Was it just feeling guilty that made him think they all suspected him of corruption? What was there to feel guilty about? About not trumpeting his suspicions aloud? His own father? He'd be a laughing-stock. Oh, for God's sake, Franco, stop beating your head in! Relax. Take things as they come. Do what's right and sleep the sleep of the just. . . .

Do what's right? Shop the old guv'nor? Stop screwing Denise? . . .

"You know what, Shorty? Why don't you pop round to the doc one evening, get him to check that ticker? It can't do any harm, and the way you're going at that hand . . . If you're not careful, you'll lose your little finger."

"Stress? If you say so, Doctor. And this feller at work says if you catch yourself rubbing your left hand and that . . . So I thought I'd best come round. I feel fine in myself, mind. I hope I'm not wasting your time. I mean I hope I am, don't I? Ha, ha."

"You know the saying 'A little knowledge is a dangerous thing'? Don't you take any notice of that friend of yours. There's nothing wrong with you, Mr. Short; you're a very fit man. Keep up the exercise, easy on the food and drink, and don't get more steamed up than you can help; you'll be right as ninepence. Tell you what, I'll give you one or two tablets. Come and see me when they're finished. Right?"

A strange doctor in a strange surgery, but the case-history in front of him. He hoped the boy knew what he was talking about.

Tablets? Bloody pills? He wouldn't have given him those if there was nothing wrong, now would he?

CHAPTER 5

BIRDS

The pills made you drowsy. Otherwise they were great. The fears
and hassles and guilts were lost. They were still there, presumably, but driven under, with iceberg peaks here and there to stop
you dropping right off.

It was in that mood and three parts asleep that he looked
through the Sûreté's report on the Botticelli.

Your request for technical examination passed to Ministry of
Fine-Arts, of which reply notes with surprise your suggestion
of doubts re authenticity. Nevertheless Minister is in princi-
ple prepared to co-operate . . . examination not possible for
several months . . . already packed for despatch to Brussels
. . . major exposition . . . palace of Fine-Arts . . . ends
month of October.

Ministry states exposition includes several major Bot-
ticellis; should attract leading international experts, and sug-
gests you obtain critical opinions there. Relevant authorities
include [God, he was tired] Professor Willison (UK), Professor Giacomelli (Florence) . . . Professor Beefburger (Har-
vard) . . . Doctor Strabismus (Utrecht) . . .

Signed, J. Clouseau, Commissar

By this time, Frank Short really was, for a moment, asleep. He
shook his head to wake himself and read it again. It wasn't

Strabismus but Straathuis; and it was Beerenberger, not Beefburger, and Commissaire Rousseau, not Commissar Clouseau, but
honestly what difference did it make? Luigi Giacomelli was the
man; if he okayed a Botticelli, that was it. Frank groaned. Keith
Billings had better not get hold of those two names or it'd mean
another limerick.

The obvious thing was to go and meet Giacomelli in Brussels.
The Guv agreed, and he wrote to make the appointment. It
would be okay, seeing that exhibition.

But here and now there was a nicer prospect still; he was gloating when he signed his letter. The evening: Denise again. Her fe-
line little body, her scent . . . All right; you're hooked. Now get
on with your work.

But the pills hadn't muzzled his conscience. And was it good
for his heart? The doctors hadn't said. Though last time he'd felt
great till old Bob got him going on his little finger. Oh, stuff it;
we only live once, and if a bird like this isn't worth living for . . .
And dying for? 'Course not. Come on, Franco boy, keep it in perspective. She's a right Doris and sensational tail, but hell . . .

His pulse rate while he waited for her was close to ninety. Not
bad, considering, and he felt a hell of a fellow in a mail-order silk
shirt he had to wear unbuttoned because that was the only way
he could get it on. . . .

"*Oaoaoah! Regarde-moi ça*, darrleeng! *Comme tu es beau!*" She
dived inside the shirt and . . . Cor! Passion or technique? Who
cared?

His pulse rate was forgotten. It must have rocketed more times
than he would have thought possible, and he put away a bottle
and a third of champagne. But when she had cleared up and
gone, with a kiss that had his guts dancing waltzes, he was feeling
great. It was the same when Teresa came back and he kissed her
and said yes, he'd had a couple of drinks in front of the telly
(and he knew all about the programmes) and actually he was on
his way to bed. He felt fine next morning too. No doubt about it,

he told himself, striding through a light warm shower under the park trees. A little of what you fancy does you good.

But it wasn't quite what he fancied after that, because his stupid Frank Short conscience got on top, and anyway he couldn't afford the champagne, so next time she came he made a proper mess of it, and the time after that he didn't even try.

"*Mais qu'est-ce que tu as, Frank?*" (What's got into you?) "You who are such a formidable lover. I don't please you any more?"

He didn't know; he just didn't know. It was like what sometimes happened with interrogation, the way, given the right sort of stress, the mind can flip, the conditioned reflexes turn inside out, and suddenly your hard-nosed villain who's stood up to everything you can throw at him for days seems to have only one thought: to cough. He'd seen it happen; although not often, and it went on being incredible.

It had to be something like that. It wasn't that she didn't turn him on, because he was drooling for her, but it was as if the wires were shorted out or something and the power supply wasn't getting where it should. So she said, "*Tant pis!*" with a Frenchified pout and shrug and sat on his knee like a pin-up in stockings and frilly knickers and kissed him modestly and talked.

And that was when it got interesting.

"Tell me, darrleeng, you are looking for those pictures from Wilton Crescent?"

"Not me. My guv'nor and some of the others. Why?" Wilton Crescent was the biggest, cheekiest, and most recent of the thefts that were driving the Guv round the bend and making him so bloody-minded it was all getting rather impossible.

"And they cannot find them? Oh, Frank! Listen, darling, I will tell you something, only you must promise never to say who told it. Promise?"

"All right then. Cross my heart!" This was giving him a very odd feeling. Okay, he was used to Franco Corti and Frank Short and their hassles, especially when Denise was around, but now it looked as if Shorty the policeman was going to get dragged in and it definitely felt odd.

"I think, Frank, if your friends were to go to Watford, there is a street there, Elmtree Rise . . ." She broke off to nibble at his mouth.

"Go on."

"Well, at number twenty-seven . . ." Her fingers started on his chest hair (black and thick; he was very proud of it). "If they were to visit number twenty-seven, then who knows? It could be interesting for them."

"What? You mean . . . ?" This was amazing.

"*Oaoaoah*, Frank! Didn't you understand? I mean what I say. If your colleagues are interested in the pictures from Wilton Crescent, they should visit number twenty-seven Elmtree Rise, Watford. But you must not tell them I said it." The fingers and the nibbling escalated. Suddenly he was Franco Corti again and it was okay.

"It's true, Guv. I swear it. A little bird definitely told me. Honest."

"I don't bloody believe it! And who says you've to come sticking your oar in? You don't know a bloody thing about it. You're not even on the bloody case!"

"Very good, Mr. Papworth. Don't say I didn't tell you." He made to go, but a bellow stopped him. "Hey, you! You cheeky little bugger! Where d'you think you're off to? By gum, we're touchy this morning, we are!" ("*By gum!*" He's said it! He's actually said it!) "What is it, lad? Time of bloody life or something? Nay, you're too young. Come on, lad, you're a chief inspector, not a wilting bloody lily. So stop acting like a nancy-boy as's fell out with his ponce and sit down. Let's have it. Tell me straight."

"I have, Mr. Papworth. Twice. I have received information, unconfirmed, from a new and reliable source I gave my word not to name, that this address would be worth a turn-over in connection with the Wilton Crescent burglary. And that's it, Guv, honest; that's all there is to tell."

"Bloody hell! All right, lad, we'll give it a spin. Get on with your work then!"

"Short speaking."

"Good afternoon, Mr. Short. This is the Silverman Gallery. Your pictures are ready for collection."

"Oh, thanks. I'll be along. How did it go then? The exhibition?"

"Oh, *super!* I mean *literally* a sell-out. Amazing!"

"Oh, that's great. Right then, Miss—er?"

"Rattray. Fiona Rattray."

"Right, then. I'll call in sometime tomorrow."

Fiona Rattray; one of the posher specimens of West End bird-life. It was always worth getting their names, you never knew. Besides, he'd a professional interest in her guv'nor. And in her? You couldn't tell. But like as not, anything iffy would go on behind her back. Or over her head, or under her innocent little nose, and she wouldn't smell a thing.

Next day he turned up about a quarter past five. There was a sort of poor man's Rubens in the window, all grapes and *vino* and bints with fat rosy bums—the new show was called *Hommages à Flandres*. Nasty provincial stuff, not his scene. Not Silverman's either, he would have thought. Perhaps it was his way of responding to the big Brussels exhibition, which was opening next week.

Inside, the only thing worth looking at was Fiona. A dish, definitely a dish: nice face, nice body, nice clothes. Oodles of class but not too snooty. Hm.

"Oh, *hello*, Mr. Short. Your pictures are downstairs; I'll get them. Would you like to pay for the landscape now?"

He sat down at her desk to write his cheque while she went for them. It was good being able to make out a kite for £350 just like that.

Meanwhile a hand covered with rings and nail-varnish appeared on the desk and a voice asked if it could help him.

"I was just writing a cheque, thanks. The young lady's bringing a couple of pictures."

"Oh, good. A satisfied customer, I hope?" The voice was upper-class like Fiona's, but with an edge that made him think perhaps it hadn't always been. "Have you got far to go?"

"Acton, actually."

"Eoh!" (Her version of *oh*. Probably didn't get a lot of customers from round there.) "Eoh, of *course!* That was your portrait Max had in the window. *Darling* Vee! *Seu* talented and such a modest child." The crimson nails matched the specs but clashed with the henna and the fussy pink blouse. The pong of money was overpowering.

He agreed with her, listening to the thumping and bumping on the basement stairs and hoping his frames weren't being ruined. "I hear the show was a success. I'm glad."

"Oh, a *great* success. Well, a *succès d'estime*. Max will almost have covered his costs. Never mind, perhaps next time he will be able to charge more realistic prices; but then one *never* makes anything from a first exhibition, does one?

Fiona had emerged, lugging the big portrait, with the landscape sketch precariously under an arm. He got up to rescue it, and met an unexpectedly shy smile. "Oh, thanks *so* much. Have you introduced yourselves? Mrs. Silverman, Mr. Short."

They were still on the first banalities when Max Silverman came out of his office. He hurried to kiss his wife. "Elsa darling! What a bonus! I thought you were at the farm."

"No. I decided to go shopping. I brought the Porsche; I thought I could run you home."

"But how sweet of you!" This was a new slant on friend Max.

Fancy doting on that old boiler! "Come on, then, let's shut up shop and go. All right, Fiona? Are you ready? Oh, hello, Mr. Short; collecting the loot? Which did you buy? Oh yes, *charming!* You won't regret it, you know; you're in on the ground floor, and if you should ever tire of it, you will bring it here, won't you? You'll be surprised what that will be worth in a year or two." Nothing about the Fra Angelico, naturally, but the friendliest of Russians. "How are you getting those home? Have you got a car? No? You'll have a dreadful job getting a taxi at this time of the day, and look, it's starting to rain. Oh Lord!"

Fiona Rattray came to the rescue. "I could run Mr. Short home in the Workwagon—that is, if I could keep it overnight. We live quite close to each other." That was news.

"Why, of course, my dear."

"That's kind of you, miss. But you mustn't go to all that trouble. I'll manage."

"No trouble at all; in fact, the other way round. *Miles* nicer than the tube. I'll get it; it's only just round the corner."

The Workwagon turned out to be a gleaming Volvo estate, and Fiona turned out to live in Chiswick. "But *only* two streets from Acton Green, *honestly!*" It was nice being driven in a big roomy car by a bird like this; for once he was glad of the rush-hour traffic. It was bad tonight, and it was nearly an hour before she pulled up in Balfour Road.

"This one? Oh, but what a *sweet* little house!" A thirties semi, just like all the others, but with a new coat of paint and the front garden at least tidy. But not little, definitely not. When they'd finished the top floor, only Sylvie and Gracie would have to share. He felt a small, Frank-Shortish flush of pride.

Teresa was out, so he asked Fiona in for a drink, but if he had a secret hope the evening would catch light, he was disappointed. She'd run out of cigarettes and he hadn't one in the house. She drank gin and tonic and admired the curtains. They talked about the garden, the traffic, Wimbledon. He liked her: her scent; her neat, athletic body; her fair-skinned, dark-browed colouring; her clear blue eyes—he liked their frankness. Very appealing.

But nothing happened, and after a second modest drink she took her leave. "Thank you *so* much, Mr. Short. I do hope we'll see you at the gallery again."

"I expect so, miss. And thanks for the lift."

A slightly awkward pause, then, "Look, do call me Fiona. Everybody does."

"I will then. And I'm Frank—some say Franco."

"Franco? I like that. 'Bye then, Franco. See you."

"'Bye, Fiona."

He escorted her to the Volvo, which was right by the gate, and she drove off. He blinked. The girl had blown him a kiss!

CHAPTER 6

GRASS

Next morning the Guv rang. "Shorty? Just step into my office a minute."

He went across, slipping on his jacket, knocked on the door, opened it and gasped. "*Gesù Maria!* Congratulations, Guv! Wilton Crescent?"

"Aye. And Cheyne Walk, Frognal, Golders Green. The lot. And d'you know who we've pulled? Skelton, Isaacson, brace or two of mugs . . ."

It was like an exhibition ready for hanging—pictures leaning two or three deep against the walls. The Stubbs was there, the Gainsborough, the Wright of Derby, the Turners, the Sickert . . .

"But that's terrific, Guv. Where were they?"

"Where yon little bird said. You've a good shout there, Shorty. Twenty-seven Elmtree Rise, Watford."

He could hardly believe it. Back at his desk he sat with his head reeling. Little sexpot Denise? His personalized supergrass? It didn't add up. Informants were criminals. They spoke the language of crime, thought its thoughts, felt its urges. Then grassed on it.

But Denise? She mightn't be all she seemed, she mightn't even be up to much good, but she was never one of those. "*Mamma mia!"* he exclaimed to Bob Wellow's empty chair. *"Mamma mia!"*

The phone again—a call for him, the girl said, from a foreign-sounding gentleman; no name. Another grass? Could be. He told her to put him on.

"Franco? I am your papà. Listen, we must meet. It is very urgent." The Italian syllables tumbled out, hushed but voluble. "We must not be seen, Franco, that is most important. Where would you suggest? It is" —cough, cough— "it is *cosa urgentissima.*"

"Okay, Papà, relax. Just give us a moment to think. Is someone watching you?"

"I think not. But—"

"Porch of the National Gallery, right?"

"No, son. Not where there are pictures."

"All right then. The Science Museum. Go by cab. Use the phone; get one to call."

"Benissimo. Straight away then. And discretion, eh?"

"Sì, Papà. Discretezza! Ciao."

Now what? he asked himself in the taxi. The old man sounded scared. If you insisted on doing business with the sort of people he dealt with, this could happen. If the old fool was in trouble, he'd probably brought it on himself, but he was still his father. So Corti to the rescue, not Frank Short. It was in the Italian marrow of him. He could no more have failed to close ranks than he could have strangled his kids. Besides, he liked the old git!

There were childhood bonds as well. He had been a tough, loutish boy, but he would sit by the hour watching and listening to his father while he worked. The skills were beyond him, but professors had envied the education. It was narrow, but it was deep, and whether he called himself Corti or Short, its roots in the Florentine bedrock were his.

Not that he thought these thoughts, waiting among the Babel

of tourists, but he felt the emotions and couldn't for the life of him think why.

His father came soon, unusually spruce in a light linen jacket, clutching a carrier-bag that turned paying off his taxi into a fumbling, gesticulating pantomime. His hair had grown enough to hide the scalp and make him almost respectable, but the anxiety was plain to see. Frank Short pushed his way forward to greet him. "*Eccomi, Papà!*" (Here I am.) "What is it then?"

The old man's damp dark eyes fidgeted across the milling faces. "A strange thing, Franchino. A package; it came in the post. Look—" He thrust forward the carrier-bag, holding it open with pudgy, nicotined fingers, the nails chewed to nothing; and Frank Short, looking down inside, saw a turf, a square of short sweet grass cut from someone's lawn.

"Strange indeed. And that's it? Just that? In a parcel?"

"And this." Antonio Corti fumbled in his pockets, each in turn, to unearth at last a muddy sheet of paper. "See?"

Using blue ballpoint, someone had drawn rather than written in large, irregular capitals: WATCH IT, MATE!

"And what are you to watch? I don't understand."

"Nor I, to begin with. But then I thought, Franco . . . *cosa mi hanno spedito?*" (What thing have they sent me?)

"*Della terra. Dell'erba.*"

"And in English?"

"Earth, Papà, and grass—*grass*, by God! *Gesù Maria! Sì, Papà*, I understand. . . ."

"Oh, you do, do you? The detective has unravelled the mystery. So perhaps now he can tell his stupid uneducated father what he should do. You know why this is, of course?"

"That newspaper rubbish presumably, the Fra Angelico and that. Someone thinks you've been telling me . . ."

"But that was weeks ago. No, Franco, I think not, it is more than that." The eyes were flicking from side to side; the head turning every few seconds to look behind.

"Papà—*discretezza*, remember? We should not stay talking here."

"True. Inside, then?"

They had to leave the carrier-bag at the cloaks, then found their way to an upstairs gallery full of spidery unintelligible contraptions, where there seemed to be no one about.

"All right, Papà? And if anyone comes, what chance is there they will know Italian?"

"*Va bene*." The walk had left the old man sweating and out of breath. "What was I saying?"

"You were saying you thought it wasn't just the thing of the Fra Angelico and your being seen to be friends with a policeman."

"True. No, son, there is a feeling about—people are frightened. There is no trust, and you know the importance of trust. Some have been arrested, others look for scapegoats. . . ."

It was true. A & A had done rather well of late; he hadn't seen the figures, but the clear-up rate must be looking good. He hadn't thought of it as anything but luck and perhaps old Titworth, who'd been there two years now and who was beginning to be respected, though he'd never be liked. Titworth was an effective policeman.

But to put it down to underworld treachery was ridiculous. There were grasses, there always had been, but no more than usual, apart from the Watford business, and that was a flash in the pan. Besides, who was left to put that down to a snout? The Guv had made a clean sweep.

Suspicious bastards, your villains. Very imaginative. Full of things about persecution. Always seeing conspiracy when there wasn't any. Convinced the courts were fixed, that prosecutions, judges, and police got together to work out the sentences if they hadn't actually primed the jury. Suckers for the wrong end of the stick. He'd seen scares like this before; they hadn't lasted, but people had got hurt, and people could get hurt now. People like Antonio Corti.

"*Capito*. There is fear about. I can see that for myself. So who, Papà? Who's putting the frighteners on you?"

"I am disappointed; I come to my son. I tell him I am suspected of betraying trust, and what does he do? He asks me to betray it! No, Franco, I could not tell you if I knew."

"You don't know? But surely you must have your suspicions?" What he wanted to say was, "You pig-headed old bastard."

"Suspicions? Suspicions? The way things are, I must suspect everyone. And in that I am not alone."

"Yes, Papà, but you will suspect some more than others. Can you give me no idea? None at all?"

Silence, the eyes all beady, avoiding his, surveying the spindly machines. The putty-coloured hands fussing in the pockets, finding a battered packet of cigarettes.

"No, Papà. No smoking, it is forbidden. Well then, what about this parcel? There was a postmark?"

"Not legible."

"And the wrapping; did you keep it?"

"Burnt."

The old man's sullenness had dignity; he could have shrunk to a petulant child, but instead he seemed to grow, to acquire the *gravitas*, of a Roman bust or a Florentine portrait. The eyes stopped running away and looked squarely into his own.

"Son, it is no use. I am not going to tell you. You are a detective; I respect your desire for knowledge of these things. But I am your father and a man of honour, and I ask you in your turn to respect that."

He did, dammit, he did! He put his arms round the old man's shoulders and kissed him on both cheeks, feeling his eyes fill. "Yes, Papà. I will respect you."

The emotional moment passed. A man and a girl in Nebraska

State University T-shirts drifted in with their arms round each other and drifted out again. The air was clammy and hot; you would have thought the exhibits would rust, they must have had some sort of treatment. . . .

Yes, but what now? "All right, you can tell me nothing. So what can I do? I cannot put a policeman on your door."

"Indeed you can not; that is the worst thing you could do. No, Franco, no police. If Antonio Corti is seen to be a man who has police protection . . . No, son."

"Not on your door, I said not. But surely, a few discreet enquiries, a presence? It would not be noticed, Papà, I promise. Not every detective has large flat feet and wears uniform boots and a bowler hat."

"Not be noticed? Franchino, do you think we are playing with children? At a time when each suspects his brother, his wife, his sons? No, son, it would be madness. Besides, how could I call myself a man of honour if I knew . . . ?"

"Who says you would know?"

"I do. You have told me yourself. Unless you were to give your word, your solemn promise, I would know. So give me that promise now. I demand it."

"But . . ."

"Your promise. If you wish to remain my son."

"Very well, my promise. You have it. So now that you have refused me information and forced me to tie my own hands, what do you desire of me? That I should perform conjuring tricks? Or call on the holy saints to destroy your enemies, or what?"

"No, son. Not the holy saints." The grey, moist face showed more than Roman *gravitas* now; it showed resolution. The family likeness was marked, though he didn't realize it, the whole aspect formidable. Not so formidable as his own when under challenge (grim and square and squat as a battle-tank; turning hard-nosed coppers suddenly nervous and he could never see why), but formidable all the same.

But there wasn't a challenge, was there? Not this time. He had volunteered, as champion, minder, and general ally, and been turned down flat.

"All right then, Papà. So what? What the hell's going on? I mean you get me out here, you act petrified; I offer to help, and you don't want to know. *Santa Maria, Papà*, what *do* you want?"

"What I want, Franco, is a son in whom I can confide, with whom I can work. I do not say one whom I can trust because that I can and do. I accept your word, I accept your love; your love and what perhaps you see as your filial duty; those I accept and cherish with affection and gratitude. But what I can never accept is your position. Franco—Franchino!—If it should ever happen that you were no longer a policeman, then . . ."

So that was it.

"Papà, no. In these things of information and of protection you have denied your son. And now it is my turn, and it displeases me more than I can say to be forced to deny my father. No, Papà; this is absolute. My work is my work, my life is my life, my responsibility is my responsibility. . . ."

"Responsibility? To place self above family, you call that responsibility? I did not teach you that, Franchino."

"But the family is not just you. There are others to consider: Teresa, Nonno, Nonna, the children. Look, I have a job, a career, a future. I am not yet forty, and already I am a chief inspector. Do you know how much I earn? A thousand pounds a month. That is good money. And in return for it I serve the most gracious Queen of the country that has been your home, Papà, for nearly forty years. They needn't have taken you, you know; they needn't have accepted you for work or residence or citizenship; they could have shipped you back to Italy, just like that. Is it irresponsible then that I should choose to serve their Queen? . . ."

"I thought you served the Greater London Council."

"Well, as a matter of fact . . . Oh, for heaven's sake, what does it matter? The point is, Papà, it is the public service. How much more responsible can a man be than to serve the public?"

The little brown eyes were quizzing him over the specs again, as if he were a freak or an alien or something. It was several seconds before the old man spoke.

"Do you know, Franco, I think you have become an Englishman. It makes me perhaps a little proud, but it is hard to accept. And *you* are hard to understand, because I shall never understand the English. But I see now that perhaps you are honourable in this, with a sort of crazy English honour, so I think I can respect you. But as for your thousand pounds a month—listen, you pay taxes, you pay insurance, you pay this, you pay that, you pay, pay, pay! A thousand a month? Zero! Why, even I, a poor, humble workman . . ."

"Don't pay a thing? No VAT, no income tax, no national insurance? All right, Papà, I don't want to know, and I don't want to know what you make. . . ."

"*Earn*, son, *earn!*"

"If you say so."

"I was going to have spoken to you of this, because it was in my mind to . . . Listen, Franchino—you know paintings; you know the art world, the market, the people. What I had hoped— and I tell you this now without desire to influence you because you have killed that—was that perhaps, if you would ever have been prepared to consider . . . which, of course, I accept freely though still with sadness you would not . . . well, if you had considered perhaps coming to work with your father and help him develop the dealing side of his business, because he is not so young as he was; and the travel, there is so much of it, and opportunities are being missed because it really ought to be international, which has always been more than I have cared to undertake. . . . If you had been prepared even to think about such things . . . I tell you one thing, Franco: You could throw your thousand a month in the Thames and never notice!"

"Oh, Papà! . . ." He felt an un-British desire to fling his arms round his father's neck and burst into tears.

"And if you were not a policeman, Franco, then you and I together—we could send these *figli di puttane* packing, eh?"

He was tempted. He really was tempted. What had that pup at the Embassy said? About Italy, about the Italians? "Survival-value, Frank, buckets of survival-value! City-states, godfathers, *condottieri*. Petty wars, petty alliances; it's like the Middle Ages. Exciting! Exhilarating! Marvellous people, Frank, every man a prince, every woman a princess! . . ."

Back to being an Italian? A prince? Back to the Middle Ages, to the world that had created Florence and its glories? Messer Franco Corti, man of the Renaissance? . . .

"Why are you rubbing your hand like that, son? Have you hurt it?"

Thump. Down to earth. Not just earth—London clay.

"No, Papà, it is just that my shirt catches and makes it tingle."

"Well, son? What about it?"

"It displeases me, and the temptations are very strong. But no. Perhaps I am already too old to change; perhaps, though I think not, I am afraid; or perhaps I have too much respect for the law, because the law of England . . . We have our arts, they have their laws, and believe me, Papà, those laws deserve respect. No, Papà, it displeases me terribly, but no."

The little eyes closed, the face sagged into a pallid, corpse-like peace. "I did not expect otherwise. But you are still my son. Listen, Franco, there must be people somewhere, not in your police but . . ."

"D'you know, I was thinking rather the same."

"I do know such men . . . well, I know of them. But not men of trust, Franco, not men of trust; that is the difficulty."

"The security firms? What about them?"

A shrug; a finger and thumb counting out invisible banknotes. "And in the end, you do not know who you are dealing with.

Men without faces, Franco, office men, climbing out of little card-indexes with numbers on their backs. I do not know how to deal with such people. So I hoped perhaps you might know of . . ."

"*Capito, Papà.* Yes, it is possible. I must have a little time to think and enquire."

"Not too much then. Thank you, Franchino. I knew you would not fail an old man."

They embraced to a sound-track of approaching feet. "Closing in five minutes. Clear the galleries, please. Closing in five minutes. . . ."

A man of trust. Who? Halfway down Balfour Road he found the answer.

CHAPTER 7

MEN OF TRUST

Sargey.

Sergeant Solomon Levine had taught Frank Short boxing and judo at school. He had been a promising welterweight, fighting around ten stone, with his eye on a Lonsdale Belt, till the war pitched him into the Commandos. He was promoted sergeant just before Dieppe, where he picked up a ruptured eardrum, a bullet in the knee, and a Distinguished Conduct Medal.

Young Frankie (he'd been Frankie at school and hadn't liked it) had idolized Sargey. He had been a good pupil, quick on his feet, with a fearsome punch but no reach, and at judo almost impossible to throw. "So you stick to judo, me lad. Forget the fight game. You'll never get below heavies, and there ain't a heavyweight in the business as won't outreach you six inches. Don't matter how good you are; you wouldn't have a chance."

Sargey had given him a lot. Not just physical skills, a mania for fitness, an old-fashioned view of duty. It was Sargey who had suggested the police in the first place. "Responsible boy like you as knows what's right; knows how to look after hisself. Just the sort they want. You could go a long way there." And it was Sargey who had served with some inspector who was mixed up with recruiting and persuaded him that even at five foot four and born in Italy, young Corti was worth a recce and they ought to make an exception. He owed a lot to Sargey Levine.

It was fifteen years since he had seen him, at the gym where he used to go to keep himself in trim and work for the judo black belt he never quite achieved. By then Sargey had got out of education (". . . no better'n Commies, them as runs it; they make me bleeding sick! Gawd knows what they're doing to poor old England. . . .") and, after an abortive shot at boxing management, had started in the security business. An outfit called Kayo, tailored for the small man, that could give the protection boys, who were becoming a headache, headaches of their own. He had a card somewhere: *KayoKare, Prop.*, S. Levine, (Sgt., R.M.), D.C.M. *"You're Okay with Kayo!"* and an address in the East End.

He found it off Cable Street, between a betting shop and a boozer, in a fragment of old Whitechapel that had escaped the blitz and the redevelopment. KAYOKARE in amateur sign-writing. A window with mortise deadlocks on a pegboard, fire extinguishers, couple of second-hand safes. Tailor's dummy with KAYOKARE armband and peaked cap, saluting. Posters announcing fights. Panel of postcard ads, no French lessons or Swedish drill, but straight. Paintwork fire-station red and police blue, very appropriate. Everything rough and ready and on the cheap but neat and clean as a kit laid out for inspection.

Open the door and it bleeps and the scanner scans you. Close it and it stops. "Morning, dear. And what can we do you for?" Earth mother, trad cockney. Goy.

"Is Mr. Levine around?"

"Arf a mo', dear." Screech: "SollEEEE!"

Dot-and-carry-one footsteps. "*Good* morning, sir. 'Ere—don't I know you?" Just the same; well over sixty but light on his feet in spite of the limp. Same ramrod back, same deadpan twinkle. Nine-tenths bald instead of just on top. The only difference really.

"Long time ago, Sargey."

"'Ullo, 'ullo; 'Sargey'? That sounds like one of my nippers.

Wait—don't tell me. . . . Why, it's young Corti. Well, I'll be . . . !" A handshake, a feint, a friendly jab in the biceps. " 'Ere, come and meet the old woman. Florrie, this is Mr. Corti. Johnnie? No, Frankie. That's right, Frankie."

"Hello, dear. What was the name then? Courty?"

"Short, actually. I changed it." Funny how that could wet-blanket a conversation.

"Yuh? Well . . . Nice to see you anyway. Let's see, wasn't it you as joined the Law? What's up then; someone been doing the nick? Come for a bit of protection? No, seriously, Frankie, how's things? Still on the Force, are you? What are you now? Sergeant? Inspector? . . ."

"Detective Chief Inspector, Art and Antiques Squad."

"Chief Inspector! You're joking! Did you hear that? Come on, Ma, stand to attention when you speak to an officer. And to what do we owe your exalted presence, *sah?*"

Frank Short told him.

"No coppers, eh? Well, I dunno, Frankie; I'm not so sure as I fancy that. I mean . . . 'ere, buzz off, Ma, this calls for a bit of man-to-man."

"Hark at him! Men, Gawd help us! All right, I'm going. Any-one like a cup of tea?"

"Yuh, why not? And shut the flipping door! Now you listen to me, young Corti. I'm not getting mixed up in nothing as ain't above-board and legal and proper, see? Ought to be ashamed of yourself coming here with a spiel like that, and you a chief bleed-ing inspector! No wonder you can't trust a copper these days, if that's the kind of game—"

"Steady on, Sargey. The old guv'nor's entitled to the protection of the law same as the rest of us. Only he won't accept it, see, or I'd give it him just like that. And if that's okay by me, I don't see why it isn't okay by you. So if you're trying to insinuate anything against me, Sergeant, by God I've a mind to ask you to step out-side!" The Guv was right; he *was* getting touchy.

"Oh, it's like that, is it? Well . . ." For about ten seconds it was eyeball-to-eyeball heavy breathing, and after the first five, Frank Short knew he was going to laugh.

They succumbed simultaneously. "You and me, Sargey? Couple of right old tearaways!"

"Gawd help us! It's them bleeding Russkies, sending out vibrations and that to confuse us. They do, you know; I seen it in the paper. All right, Frankie, you're on. But it's not easy, mind. Costs a lot of money—I mean the wages for a start, and what with overheads and bank interest and the lot, I can double that and still work for nothing less VAT."

"How much then? Roughly?"

"Depends what we do, dunnit? Let's say I put a man to live in; good men don't come cheap, and I don't use rubbish. All right, he's prepared to be reasonable about overtime, but he still wants time off, and that means a relief. You're into a couple of hundred a week before you start, and that's just wages. Double it and it's four, and I'm working for nothing. I'd want five off of most customers."

"I see what you mean. Mind you the old guv'nor's not short of a bob, but that sort of money . . . I dunno, Sargey. I mean maybe for a week or two, but what good's that? . . ."

"All right, so the old geezer can't afford it, or not for long. We're down to part-time then. Is his gaff secure?"

"I doubt it. I don't go there a lot in case someone starts jumping to conclusions."

"Started, ain't they?"

"Yes. He'll want his premises seen to."

"D'you want me to look after that? Not as you couldn't do it yourself."

"I'll ask him. What's it going to cost? Two or three hundred?"

"Bit more than that. It depends how far you go. Front door, back door, window locks, a simple alarm. The right side of a thousand, anyway."

"You won't need window locks; they're solid. He's never had one open in his life."

"'Course if you start on the fancy stuff, the sky's the limit. Thousands."

"You know what? The three of us want to get together."

Where better than the Trattoria Vaccarino? In the alcove at the back by the kitchen stairs that was usually kept screened. One o'clock. A little private lunch for three.

It was two before they got down to the menu. Drinks had to be stood, staff to be chatted up, Nonno and Nonna to be embraced, and Sargey to be introduced to them all. Including Hector Dando.

It was not many months since Ettore Dando, former sergeant from *polizia* records in Rome, eurocommunist, "good friend" of the British Embassy and victim of right-wing faction, had arrived with a *please* from Special Branch, looking for work. Since he had done Frank Short proud and been rewarded with a bloody nose, three broken ribs, and a posting to Sardinia, Frank Short had bullied and blackmailed the family to take him, and since some sort of funnies were paying, he had won.

So Dando had taken over the books from Teresa.

He was willing. He was versatile. Before long he was indispensable. His English was coming on fast; he had dropped the "Ettore" within a month ("They don't know to say it") and insisted on "Hector."

A pale, bespectacled thirty-two-year-old, well set up, Latin-dark, a fastidious dresser with a taste for white worn with trousers of shop-window crispness. A flat in Camden town, a mouse-coloured little wife, three small daughters, and that was it. Except for the party card, but that was SB's affair.

It was two before he brought the menu. He waited on them himself, like a professional, and though it would probably have been safe to talk in his presence, there were some silences when he appeared. Not always. Not all the talk was business.

Antonio Corti to Sargey's good ear, for example, in his slow, uncomfortable English. "You were soldier then? That is good; I also was soldier. You fight much battles?"

"Nah. Only one. Fifteen or sixteen hours. Quite enough, that was."

"Ah. At me was same. One day fight, tomorrow finish, no more fight." He really was spruced up, wearing a tie, which was unheard of—a shiny brown one, very new and up-to-the-minute.

"Wounded, was you?"

"No. Was prisoned. Was much disfortune. In Libya, in desert with lorries; no petrol, no bullets, no officers, too much sand, too much hot. We are hundred fifty men and suddenly, *grrrrmmmmm!* Fifty, hundred English tanks; we can do nothing. All prisoned. War finish."

"Can't win 'em all, can you. What mob was you? Infantry? Artillery? . . ."

"No, no. Transportation. And you?"

"Infantry. Well, Marines. Commando, actually."

A gracious nod to an equal in valour. "You were not afraid?"

" 'Course I was."

"I was not afraid." Was that a lie? Or just fooling himself? Or even the truth? Frank Short felt irritated, affectionate, and protective all at once.

As for business, Sargey was clearly accepted as a man of trust. A deal was negotiated and agreed. A resident bodyguard till the premises had been checked and made secure—forty-eight hours maximum and after that at night only—and by day spot checks from the street, with a simple code, a jug on a window sill, the only decorative object in the house except for the pictures; right for okay, centre for suspicious, left for SOS.

The phone was better, and KayoKare had radio contact with its men, so the jug code was only a reserve. And slow, Frank Short was thinking as they reached agreement over coffee and grappa (no grappa for Sargey, whose only drink was a half of light ale from the pub). Anyway, that was it for a month.

And the money? Special rates for an old friend's father. A thousand, covering the first four weeks, plus the cost of any work on the building. No little *disconto* for cash? Ah well, such is life. Time and method of payment then? "Ah! Excuse." Papà Corti searched his pockets for wads of much-put-upon tenners, to be counted among the cups and glasses with great coughings and gruntings, and divided into stacks, of which the larger had to be redistributed among the pockets before the smaller could be handed to Sargey with a princely flourish. After which the old man vanished to the loo.

"Well, Sargey. What do you reckon?"

"Rum old geezer, innee? Well, you tell me. I'll do what I can, naturally, but I can't guarantee results. I mean how could I? . . ." He went off with old Corti to inspect the premises and Frank Short buttonholed Hector Dando.

"Ettore un momento, per favore . . ."

"Please, kindly speak English. This way I learn it."

"All right then. Hector, I wonder if you can help me. Didn't you say you'd a cousin at Carabinieri HQ?"

"Please? HQ?"

"Headquarters." A pause while it went down in his notebook. Under "Abbreviations," no doubt, and in correct alphabetical order.

"Is true. He is a clerk, not a carabineer."

"Would he be able to look into something for me, an ordinary police matter? Well, not quite ordinary, a little sensitive, so I have to be careful. Like my father would say, *discretezza*, eh?"

"I understand. Is possible I could help you. What is the query, please?"

"Count Eugenio delle Bandenere lives in Monte Carlo. I want to know about him. Background, really: age, family, life-style.

Profession if he has one. Any police record, though there's no reason why there should be. For what it's worth, I'm looking into some pictures that might be forgeries, and two seem to have belonged to him. It's sensitive because one of them was acquired by a very exalted person, so . . ."

"So it is sensitive. Understood."

"Mind you, we don't know if they're forgeries or not, but we should before long; and if so, then a recent owner . . . Get it?"

"Certainly. I get it."

"That's all, really. Point is, I don't want to go through official channels."

A broad smile; Hector's smile was endearing. "I get it. I will enquire for you. In confidence. But perhaps not the cousin of the carabineers; I have others. Count Eugenio delle Bandenere, that is right?"

"That's right. *Ciao*, then, Hector. And thanks."

He hurried guiltily to the Yard, guilty of using all that firm's time on his own business, guilty of eating all that food and drinking all that drink. If he went on like that, it'd be another heart attack, and next time he mightn't be so lucky.

The walk through the park helped a little. He was dripping all over his desk when he picked up the first letter in the tray.

His mood vanished. The letter was in Italian. From Professor Giacomelli in Florence, posted a week ago. The Professor would be in Brussels till . . . Good grief! He'd be there till tomorrow.

CHAPTER 8

MUSSELS AND CHIPS

Frank Short was getting tired of explaining he was Italian; it had been less trouble being called Corti.

"*Capito*," said Professor Giacomelli. "Understood. I did not expect to meet a fellow-Florentine. What convenience, because my English—I can read it, naturally, but to speak . . ."

They were struggling through the crowd that choked the Palais des Beaux Arts. It clung three deep round the least of the exhibits. It queued four abreast along the pavement of the Rue Royale and round the corner two hundred yards back and down the steps to the side-door where the coach parties scrummed and sweltered.

Frank Short was glad he didn't get claustrophobia. The galleries were below ground and without daylight. The ceilings weren't that high, and free-standing walls divided the rooms into cramped, packed spaces where the merest glimpse of a picture was a triumph. It was ten minutes before they found the Botticelli and five more before they got where they could see it. Lorenzo delle Bandenere, flanked by a Raphael prelate and a Giovanni Bellini doge, inspected them with confidence. He looked right enough to Frank Short.

"Well, *Professore?*"

Giacomelli stared back at the picture, making faces and twitching slightly. To look at, he could have been a clerk or small official—a slight, greyish man in glasses with a balding head and lanky hair with half-hearted drake's tails on his neck. He answered with a question.

"How old would you say he is?"

"Forty? Forty-five?"

"Or younger? They aged quicker in those days. Can we put him at thirty-five?"

"If you say so."

"No younger; certainly no younger. *D'accordo?*"

"Agreed."

"Hm." The Professor was biting his nails now. "Now Botticelli was in Rome in 1481. . . ."

Frank Short remembered the fresco on the south wall. "Sistine Chapel?"

Giacomelli nodded, unimpressed. "This Lorenzo delle Bandenere. Not much is known about him, except that he was Francesco delle Bandenere's son. Francesco was born in 1430, that we do know. So work it out. . . ."

Mental arithmetic wasn't Frank Short's thing. He was still struggling when Giacomelli's sharp voice resumed. "If Lorenzo was thirty-five in 1481, he was born when his father was sixteen. Likely?"

"No. But possible, surely?"

"I think not. Francesco's wife was younger still. Two years? Three? I forget . . ."

They married young in those days, but Frank Short got the point. Except: "But why 1481, *Professore?*"

"Ah. The Bandenere were foreigners. Soldiers of fortune in the early quattrocento; then Francesco settled near Tivoli. That is close to Rome. They were hangers-on of Naples and the Borgias. They had land. They did not move about. I think that if Botticelli were to paint Lorenzo, it would be in Rome. So 1481."

"Oh."

"I take it it is established that this *is* Lorenzo delle Bandenere?"

Lorenzo's calm eyes told him not to be stupid. A tall boy with cream-coloured hair was trying to force his way in front of Frank Short while talking loudly in German. Frank Short stood on his toe and said, "No one's questioned it as far as I know. The picture came from the Bandenere family."

"And where did the provenance come from? Certainly there is this letter from Botticelli to Lorenzo asking for payment, but it is dated, if I remember, 1478."

"But you say he painted him in 1481? . . ."

"Exactly. So I would regard that letter with suspicion, *Ispettore*. Especially as its present whereabouts are not, I think, known. Then this nineteenth-century Cunningham. Who was Cunningham? I don't know. Does anyone know?"

The letter describing the two pictures in the Villa Bandenere had begun, *Dear Ruskin*, and had appeared on the London market as "the property of a gentleman" not long before Count Eugenio sold the pictures to Silverman. It had gone to a California university, and Carrozza's photocopy was in Frank Short's pocket.

"Good question," he answered. "I thought perhaps you . . ."

Giacomelli shook his head. "I am no nineteenth-century scholar, but those who are have expressed doubts. I made some enquiries, you see, when you wrote to me. . . ."

"So what we have is a picture which is doubtful on chronological grounds, supported by an equally doubtful provenance. Right, *Professore?*"

"That is so."

"And on critical grounds?"

Giacomelli started twitching again. The Nordic boy had been replaced by a dark-skinned child, probably female, who reeked of sweat and peppermint.

"Critically and aesthetically, *Ispettore*, it is what one would expect from Botticelli at that period: typically linear treatment, indeed all the characteristics. A very pleasing little panel, very *simpatico*, and this causes me, I admit, to doubt my own doubts a little. *Finalmente*, who can say? Without laboratory examination it is impossible to be sure, and even then . . ."

That was all he could get out of him. Doubts, then doubts about doubts, none of which was news. The picture looked right, or it would never have been bought and sold as such, but increasingly it didn't smell right. And if this one was wrong, then the sensitive Piero di Cosimo was probably wrong too, and if they were both wrong and from Maxwell Silverman International, London, and the Piero di Cosimo had been restored in tempera, then Antonio Corti . . . grrr!

"And now, *Ispettore*, what are you doing about lunch? Do you know Brussels?"

"First time. I got here this morning."

"Ah. Then I will show you where to go. We will eat together."

"Thank you. I'd like that. Do you think I've time to try and get round a bit first?"

It was an important show, tracing the antecedents of the Mannerist and Venetian schools. He ploughed in, with the Professor patiently at his heels. After two rooms he was wilting, in the third he was defeated. He turned to say so to the Professor, and found him shaking hands with a man in a denim suit and a panama hat. Gervase Willison.

"Why, Fwank! But how delightful! Is it business or pleasure?"

"Business, I'm afraid. It seems there's a picture here could be wrong. Professor Giacomelli's been kind enough to—"

"Don't tell me, let me guess. Oh, but *yes*; definitely yes. The Bandenere Botticelli, *surely*? *Such* an unconvincing provenance; don't you think so, Luigi?"

"Please? My English . . ."

Willison tried again, in Italian on a par with Giacomelli's English.

"*Certamente.* The provenance must be extremely suspect. And now lunch; you will join us, *caro collega mio?* Shall we walk? It is good for the appetite."

Brussels was grey. It had been noticeable in the taxi from the Gare du Nord (in a fit of economy the Guv had made him take the night ferry to Ostend), and it was noticeable now. Grey stone, grey concrete; they walked through an incoherent web of streets on dark granite setts. A grimy Gothic cathedral frowned over a sprawl of public gardens crisscrossed with traffic, their lurid, angular flower beds interspersed with equally lurid petrol stations.

"This city has no soul," Giacomelli said in English.

"Oh, but it *has*, Luigi. Their little Manneken Pis. Isn't that what they must think of us all? And who can blame them? The cockpit of Europe, Fwank; everyone *always* bwings their wars to Belgium; and now it's Eurocwats and Eurocapital and Euro-tourists like ourselves. What else *can* the poor dears think? . . ." His *r*'s were better today; he wasn't caricaturing himself.

The Grand-Place needed a bath and a change of clothes. All that opulent carving looked grubby, irrelevant, depressing. Frank snorted gently at it and allowed himself to be led into a pedestrian alley with a jaw-cracking Flemish name, which the others called the *Petite rue des Bouchers* and which was solid with restaurants from end to end.

The depression lifted. Was the soul of Brussels here? Or was it split like his own, half Flemish, half French? Big deal.

The restaurant was ethnic and friendly. The thing to eat was mussels and chips; they were on every menu in the street. He began to enjoy himself.

"Inspector!" The voice was unmistakable; effortless, resonant, smooth. "What a very small world! I saw you through the window. Why, it's Professor Willison, isn't it? Maxwell Silverman. And this is . . . ? *Professore!—Onorissimo!* You are here for the exhibition, no doubt, like the rest of us. Likewise the great detective? Or is it business, Inspector?"

He had to think quick. Keep the Botticelli out of it, and he'd never get away with a lie. "Business, actually. I'm not free to say what." He repeated that in Italian to make sure. But he could imagine Silverman's thoughts: exhibition . . . Art and Antiques Squad . . . Botticelli expert. Two plus two equals four: portrait of Lorenzo delle Bandenere. There was nothing he could do about it, so he might as well enjoy his lunch.

Then Willison had to invite the man to join them.

"Oh, that *is* nice of you. I had booked at the Maison du Cygne, but my guest had to cry off, and really, one doesn't care to lunch at that level on one's own, so I thought I'd take potluck among the tourists. Now then; what are you all eating? *Moules frites?* Excellent. *Garçon, encore des moules, s'il vous plaît, et encore une bouteille.* What a pity one doesn't speak Flemish; the waiters are all Flemings, you know. . . ."

Frank and Max watched each other surreptitiously through the meal, and whatever Silverman might be thinking about him, Frank knew what he was thinking about Silverman. Max was worried.

There was some satisfaction in that, but it wouldn't make his job any easier. He sat like a quiet little bull, frowning over his Muscadet and mussels and chips, leaving the others to sort out their language problems the best they could. He had difficulties enough of his own. Must ring Kayo.

The mussels were delicious, and he must have dunked half a loaf in the liquid. So was the Muscadet. He ordered a third bottle on the strength of it, then tucked into his salad and the cheeseboard and a Homeric wedge of *gâteau*, and started worrying about his heart. . . .

"And how's your tweasure, Fwank? Did you know Fwank's got a tweasure? A Fwa Angelico, no less . . ."

He swore inwardly.

"Now what makes you say that?" Max Silverman, large, urbane, and relaxed, had stopped patronizing them and turned into quite good company. Doubts formed in Frank Short's mind. Could he be wrong? Was it just prejudice, plus resentment at being shown the door that time in the gallery? Suddenly it seemed possible the man was honest, or at least legitimate. ". . . I've inspected that picture myself, and to be sure it's very nice indeed, but the provenance . . ."

Was there a flicker? As if he wished he hadn't used that word?

"No pwovenance at all, Max, but one does have an eye. A *feel*. One can say in all modesty that over the years one develops a feel for these things. Haven't you a feel? Of course you have. And I'm certain Luigi has. An *informed* feel, naturally . . ."

Frank Short thought crude thoughts about Gervase Willison and informed feels. All the same, he was a nice guy, actually, and he believed him about the Fra Angelico. So did Max Silverman, but he wanted it, so he was bound to knock it. He reverted to his quiet-bull mood and paid his whack (which made his hair stand on end; it was more than twenty pounds, and the restaurant was modest). Then he phoned London and was answered by Florrie Levine, who could tell him nothing, and set off in the afternoon heat to walk some calories out of his system.

The cathedral set him brooding about himself again. It was forbidding in there, the stonework black with dirt, with safety nets to catch bits of falling vault. If the soul of Brussels was here, heaven help it. No statues, no candles, no colour; just grim, neglected stone. He thought it must be Protestant at first, but it wasn't. It was unlike any Catholic church he had seen.

Northern Europe, said the greyness; you ought to appreciate this. This is your sort of church, Frank Short.

Depressed, with a hangover from lunch, he caught the boat train to Ostend.

CHAPTER 9

INFORMANT SPADGER

Next morning he walked straight from Victoria to the Yard. Bob Wellow was there already, looking like a canny old country doctor on the box. "Morning, Shorty. Have a good trip?"

"Not specially. You can't sleep properly on those ferries, and I've got a headache."

"Old ticker taking it all right?"

"You ought to have been a doctor, hadn't you? Oh, it's not too bad."

"You want to blow off steam, Shorty. It's the ones as sit brooding and worrying, or go at everything like a bull at a gate. The ones as are permanently frustrated. A little of what you fancy never hurts, you know . . ."

Remember Papà? When I said Teresa would think I was with a woman? "Perhaps you should be with one. A change can do a man good." A little of what you fancy? Denise? Stop feeling guilty, man. Another heart attack would hurt Teresa more than me having a bit on the side. That'd go down a treat at confession. He waded into his overflowing in-tray with a sigh.

He couldn't concentrate. He would read something three times and not know what it was. Admin, case reports, lists of stolen goods, none of it seemed real. None of it seemed to matter. What mattered was his father, Sargey, Denise. Family. Home.

His lovely Fra Angelico. And with a sort of second-hand reality because they could so easily connect with his father, the Bandenere portrait and the Piero di Cosimo *Diana,* and Brussels and Giacomelli and Hector Dando.

This was a waste of time. He grunted and went out. The third phone box worked, but the sun was full on it: If you opened the door, you couldn't hear; if you closed it, you melted. Situation normal. He dialled his father.

All well, thank heaven; the doors were fitted up, windows checked, the alarm nearly finished. The day guard was getting ready to leave.

Denise next. He wondered where she lived. She wouldn't tell him, and foreign, suspicious voices would answer the phone, a new one every time. He'd been tempted to put on his policeman's hat and find out, but it would have been dishonourable. Besides, he wasn't sure he wanted to know.

This morning the voice was a woman's. Unreachable. No English at all. "Verdier! Denise Verdier!" he repeated for the tenth time, the replies having varied from an unidentifiable quacking gabble to dead silence. "Denise Verdier!" Silence again; then footsteps, heavy breathing, and eventually a male voice, hostile. "What you want?"

"May I speak to Denise Verdier, please?"

More silence. Footsteps came and went on concrete stairs. A baby cried and was shouted at; somewhere a long way off oriental pop music whined and rhythmed. Earl's Court? Notting Hill? Could be anywhere really. . . .

"Verdier."

"Denise! I'm back. Are you free tonight? . . ."

She was. He could get through the day now.

He hadn't known how tired he was till that evening: Afterwards all he wanted to do was sleep. He was a quarter conscious, flat on his back, with Denise in the crook of his arm, when her voice insinuated itself into his mind.

"Frank, was that nice? I pleased you?"

"Mmmmm . . ."

"Would you like to hear another secret?"

"Mmmmm . . ."

"Frank! *Écoute!* Wake up." Her fingers walked across his body to the exact spot, and he woke with a gentle, pleasurable twitch.

"Yes? What was all that?"

"A secret, Frank. You would like to hear one?"

"Yes. Why not?"

"There was some silver, *des flacons, des chopes.* . . . It belonged to Lord Harborough."

"Oh yes?" There'd been a break-in three weeks back.

"Well, Frank, there is this person they call Scouse. . . ."

"Scouse Blamey?" There wasn't a copper in London who didn't know that name, and most of them were gunning for him. A stroppy, violent Liverpool buck, who fancied himself a collector.

"Frank, if you were to look where I shall tell you. . . . Kiss me, Frank. Not there, here. *C'est ça! Oaoaoah!*" This wasn't a little of what he fancied, it was a mountain.

"Frank. Those paintings at Watford. There was to be a reward?"

"I suppose so. Yes. I hadn't thought."

An incredulous little laugh. "*B'en alors?* So?"

"So why not? Yes. Great."

"How much would it be, Frank?"

One or two of those pictures were in the six-figure bracket, and the lot must add up to three quarters of a million. So if only half were insured and for only half their value, that was nearly two hundred thousand. And at 10 per cent, which was the going rate, that meant fifteen or twenty grand. "Dunno," he said. "Five or ten thou?"

"Oh, *Frank!*" She hurled herself on top of him and kissed his face all over like an enthusiastic puppy.

"There's one thing, though. They'll want to know all about you."

"*Oaoaoah! Mais . . .*"

"Wait for it. It doesn't have to be gazetted. But someone's got to know, haven't they?"

"But you know. Isn't that enough?"

"Know? I know your name; I know you're French; I know you were with Fred, and that's it. I don't even know your address. Listen, sweetheart, if you're going to get that money, they'll want more than that."

"But . . ."

"Like I say, nothing gets published. But I have to know. Me and one very senior officer, that's all."

She hesitated. He couldn't see her face but guessed it had aged. "*B'en.* If that is what I must do . . ."

She was from Paris, a squalid working-class suburb; father unknown, mother on the game. It was the same desperate, fatherless, half-starved wartime infancy as his own, but afterwards instead of a father and a new life, a mother going steadily to bits and having to cope by herself. Somewhere she'd picked up a bit of dancing; at twelve she was hoofing it in down-market nightspots and dreaming of ballet school. At fourteen she was a stripper, sleeping with the *patron*—it was him or the customers— and mother was in an institution.

And that had been her world. She'd climbed a little way up the ladder, earned quite good money, had some quite good times. And then married Jules Verdier, who brought her to swinging London in 1969, when the smiles were getting a little fixed, for a juicy West End booking that turned out to be a particularly nasty strip club, and vanished with the loot.

Denise, being a trouper, carried on. Dancing, stripping, a bit of modelling, a bit of sleeping around (for companionship or a roof, but never, "nevaire," for cash—at least that was what she said). Fred Bugler had fallen for her when she was posing for a life class at the Gibbonsian, and those years as his third wife in all but name had been her best.

Then, last year, disaster, and Fred had thrown her out; she thought for her own sake.

Frank Short believed her, more or less, and got chapter and verse where he could, so it wouldn't be just her word. Her current address was indeed in Notting Hill, but he had to promise to keep clear before she would give it to him.

He said, "You'll need a *nom de plume*, for the files. Anything you fancy? A man's name, English, Eskimo? You name it."

"Sparrow. Can it be Sparrow? No—Spadger. The good cockney, yes?"

"Okay. Spadger then."

"*B'en alors*. Well then, Frank, apropos of Mister Scouse; where one should look is just on the mantelpiece of his flat—it is in Dulwich, where he calls himself Morrison, number . . ."

They looked there when Blamey was out, and found a very nice quart-sized covered tankard, hallmarked "London 1674," the property of the seventh Baron Harborough. They left it where it was in case they upset anyone, and with the help of some smart detective work by DS Billings, K, they collected the lot apart from Blamey, who had, in Billings's words, gone walkies. Lord Harborough's insurance policy was indexed and his brokers were offering sixty-five hundred pounds reward. At A & A, Shorty's snout was story of the month.

Funny. He'd always had the feeling she was up to something. Well, it was okay by him. Though where she'd got her information was, in her own words, *autre chose*.

Next day at the Yard he checked what he could and wrote his confidential memo.

. . . After a chance meeting, found informant had criminal connections, though not involved or engaged actively in crime.

Subsequently cultivated informant, who volunteered information on 19 May last which led to the arrest of John Skelton, David Isaacson, and others, and to recovery of property to the insured value of £168,880, and subsequently further information which led to the recovery of antique silverware worth £65,073 (Lord Harborough) from premises rented by D. I. Blamey, though not as yet to an arrest.

It appears that this information was provided in the knowledge of the rewards (10% of insured value of property recovered) offered by the various assessors under the usual conditions.

Enquiries reveal that she was not involved in the commission of any of the offences, and I ask that she be suitably rewarded.

He sealed his memo in an envelope, marked it CONFIDENTIAL, INFORMANT SPADGER, and took it to Papworth. "There you are, Guv. I said it was a little bird as told me!" The joke fell flat. Papworth didn't like being kept in the dark. He received the envelope with formal reserve and a face of contained fury.

"Very good, Chief Inspector; here is your receipt. You are familiar with the procedure—I will personally hand this envelope to a deputy assistant commissioner, who will get in touch with the insurers, and in due course a commander or above will ask you to arrange a meeting with your informant, at which he will personally deliver the rewards on their behalf."

Honestly, life on the Force these days . . . DACs and commanders having to waste time on insurance rewards. Ought to be thinking about insurance himself. His Fra Angelico; the other pictures too. And security—get Balfour Road made safe. Get Kayo on to it; all it needed was a phone call.

Did his father have any insurance? His finances were a mystery. Those wads of dog-eared tenners . . . And tax? The Inland Revenue must know he was there. The thought of a tax form filled in by Antonio Corti was mind-boggling.

And if the old codger were to snuff it (that cough?) was there a will?

His father did have this dear and valued client who was also an accountant, so he had professional advice of a kind, though what kind? The mind boggled again. But one of these days there'd be death duty. And a fair bit left? Something to retire on perhaps, or start his own business? Or go into partnership with Sargey? There'd be a good market for a detective-cum-security outfit that knew the art scene.

His father was a worry. His safety; the Botticelli; the Piero di Cosimo. A faker who could stand a chance against a full examination by the Gruenwald was rare. Underpainting for a start, good or bad, because mostly in fakes there wasn't any. Then damage, faked repairs, faked old varnish; everything done and removed and the restorations repainted, and in tempera. No faker he had heard of would do all that. But Antonio Corti might. That kind of sly perfectionism was in his character. And he had the skills. Typically, if you X-rayed a fake, you got a hesitant outline, paint built thick along edges where the drawing had been constantly corrected. It needed a draughtsman of calibre to get it right first time and not muck it about. Antonio Corti drew very well indeed.

But was he a faker at all? These two pictures apart, his thing was restoration. Creative restoration, if you like, but he needed an existing painting to work on. After all, there was only the workmanship and Silverman to connect him with those two pictures, and who said there wasn't some mute inglorious van Meegeren somewhere? Anywhere—it didn't have to be England or even Europe. Your meticulous Oriental would make a first-class faker. So doubtless would a little green man from outer space. He shrugged and got on with his paperwork.

"Millions? Little picture like that? You're joking." Sargey Levine, seated in one of the chairs of the Shorts' new three-piece suite, sipped his light ale.

"I keep telling him," said Teresa, perched on the edge of the settee in a charcoal skirt and dove-grey blouse. "If I've told him once, I've told him a hundred times." (She had.) "He ought to sell it. He'll have to pay tax but he'll still make a fortune. And he won't have all this worry and bother. You don't know what it's doing to him, Mr. Levine. . . ."

"Oh, come on, make it Solly."

"Solly then. I mean just think what we could do with the money . . ."

"But it isn't just the money," Frank Short said, "is it, darling? Trouble is, Sargey, it's in my blood. I can't help it; I'm hooked. I mean letting that picture go now as I've got it, it'd be like losing a limb. And it isn't as if we're short—sorry, that wasn't a joke—I mean the pay these days. . . . And Teresa doesn't do that bad, do you, darling? She gets good commission, and the Trattoria's a profitable little business."

"Don't tell me. You're loaded. What about a silent alarm then? One as makes a 999 call."

"Central Station job? That makes sense."

"Cost you a couple of hundred more, mind, but after that, less than two pound a week. That's over and above what you'd pay for a bell system. It's not a lot when you think what that picture's worth."

It wasn't. He settled for that, actuated by external and internal doors, with an air-pressure switch in the lounge and a pressure mat under the Fra Angelico.

After that it was door and window locks. "Right, Frankie, that's it. Start work Monday." (This was Wednesday.) "Though you'll have to wait a week or two for the outside line . . ."

He hoped it would be okay; he'd had the picture six months and it had been public knowledge for a good three weeks; two or three more shouldn't hurt, but he'd sleep easier when it was done.

"And what about the old guv'nor?" he asked. "All quiet?"

"Quiet, yes; but there's just a couple of things . . ." Sargey hesitated, glancing at Teresa, who remembered urgent business in the kitchen. "Yuh. Well, it's like this, see. Point one, he's got a bird."

"Has he, by God? Not . . . ?" An awful foreboding grew in him. "What's she like?"

"Little shrimp of a thing, blond, about four foot ten. Foreigner."

He managed to keep his cool. "The old devil. Having it off, are they?"

A shrug. "Doesn't stay all night, if that's what you mean. And the boy as goes there nights hasn't seen any snogging or anything. Don't come on till nine, though, does he? Dunno, Frankie."

"Ah well. It's nice to know. Let's hope when I'm his age . . ."

"Now, now! You're a married man, me boy." It was only half a joke; Sargey was rather strait-laced.

"But there's something else, Frankie. You know the old geezer said no coppers?"

"Yes."

"Well, you haven't been up to anything, have you? Cos there's others besides my boys watching that gaff, see, and we know as it's Bill. Young Johnny—bright lad that, he was on the Force himself—young Johnny recognized one of them. So I ask you again, Frank Short: Have you been going behind my back? Because if you have . . ."

"For God's sake, Sargey! Why should I do a thing like that? No, it's not our firm; not Art and Antiques, I swear it."

"Who is it then?"

"I dunno. But I'll damned well find out. Did you get his name —the one your man recognized?"

"I did. Hang on a minute." A notebook appeared. "'Ere we are. Bagshaw, Stewart Bagshaw, right?"

Detective Stewart Bagshaw, Frank Short found out next day, worked for CIB2. Also, and this might or might not be coincidence, CIB2 was one of the departments Chuck Carrozza had been going to visit on his study tour. CIB2 was the rubber-heel mob, part of the Complaints Investigation Bureau, and its job was smelling out corrupt policemen.

CHAPTER 10

DANCING

Frank's first instinct was to storm in on Titworth and demand explanations. But Titworth probably knew nothing about it, and Titworth's declared trust in him mightn't survive. Leave it, he told himself. You're clean. Leave it alone. Though, looking at it from the rubber-heel angle, was he that clean? Not if they'd sussed old Papà.

And now it was an obbo. Which meant suspicion. Which made his father a suspected criminal. And this suspected criminal had given him presents. Which would lead to more suspicion. Vicious circle.

Right then, Franco boy, what can we do about it? Sod-all. Why does he do these things? He doesn't need the money. The way he lives he could do it on an old age pension. So he subsidizes the kids. Me too, I suppose; but hell, we're not poverty-stricken. And then I find he's carrying on with my woman. Two-timing little scrubber.

Santa Maria! That info: the Watford pictures, Blamey, the Harborough silver. It's him! No wonder he gets parcels of grass. They'll be on to her next, and that won't be funny. Silly bitch. Treating it as a kind of game. She won't know what hit her.

This has got to stop. Or has it? What copper in his right mind would kill a snout like that? Kill? Not literally. Could get literal if you don't stop her. A snout like that? You take risks to get information of this class; and if it was just her . . . Only it isn't, it's your own father. Your own father's life. No way you put that at risk, Franco Corti. No way.

Scrubber! On to a good thing, isn't she? Twisting the old fool round her itty bitty finger. He'll be on his knees with a ring and a bunch of roses next.

The nightmare completed itself. Marriage! Not just to Antonio Corti but to a fortune. Tax-free to his wife. A fortune in dog-eared tenners, but mostly in pictures that by rights would have come to him, to Gino, Ches, and little Tony, perhaps even Sylvie and Gracie. She'd have it off him! Before he died, like as not, so the courts couldn't touch it, which they might if it was after death . . .

Frank Short bent over his desk, laid his head on his arms, and cried.

"Come in, Mr.—er, Short. Take a seat. Coronary spasm, wasn't it? Ah yes, last July. And a fortnight ago I gave you some tablets. Keeping fit, are you? Come for some more?"

"Well, yes, I suppose I have. But . . ."

"Something wrong?"

He puffed down his nose. "You can say that again."

"Ah. And what appear to be the symptoms?"

"Panic. Fury. Frustration. Fragmentation. Disintegration . . ."

"Ah yes. It's known in the trade as life. Gets like that, doesn't it? Anything specific?"

"Well, I get these headaches, and then the indigestion. And that funny feeling in my hand—the pills don't seem to stop it al-together."

"I see. Well, let's have a look at you."

"Well, Mr. Short. I'd say you're as fit as a horse. (What sort of a horse, for pity's sake?) You're taking plenty of exercise? Not over-doing things?"

"No." He'd been very modest lately about the food and drink.

"What's the trouble then? Stress?"

He nodded, then blurted, "This feller at work says I want to blow off steam. Relax and that."

"Sensitive chap. Tell me, Mr. Short—I see your card used to be in a different name. If it isn't impertinent, may I ask where your family came from?"

"Italy, actually. I was born in Florence."

"Ah. That's interesting. Did you know that in Italy the incidence of cardiac disease is exceptionally low? Don't ask me why. Diet perhaps, life-style, emotional habits . . ."

This was news to him. "Go on."

"Now this is pure speculation, because I don't know the background . . . one rather wonders if in changing your name you hoped to throw off your Italian origins and become an Englishman. Am I right?"

"I suppose so."

"Hm. An uptight, inhibited, constipated Englishman? Well, Mr. Short, if you want to increase the pressures in your life and wire down the safety-valves, you're making a first-class job of it."

"Bloody hell, Doctor! This is nothing to do with that. That's a totally different problem." Steady, Franco boy, don't go losing your temper. You *are* getting stroppy these days.

"But we still need our safety-valves, don't we?"

Safety-valves. Denise? Like hell Denise was a safety-valve. She had been, till she turned into the bloody problem.

"So think about it, Mr. Short. And meanwhile I'll give you some capsules—nothing ferocious, just a gentle hint to the blood pressure. And do try to take things a bit easier, right? Good night then. Next, please."

It was a palliative. He slept well that night, drawing comfort from Teresa, who let him snuggle his back against her and nuzzled his neck. Up at six sharp. Exercises, their coffee, his kipper;

the fetid scrum of the tube in time to walk from Hyde Park Corner.

The park was rich with June, the morning fresh with a light North Sea breeze. A champagne morning to turn a man into a boy. He ran fifty yards just for the joy of it, and for a few precious minutes his troubles left him.

But not for long. The morning, or the capsules, or Teresa had cooled his head, and instead of panic there was a sense of challenge. Of honourable combat against enemies worth a serious man's attention.

Enemy number one, Denise. Two, whoever was putting the frighteners on his father. Three, though he wasn't sure why, Max Silverman. Four, CIB2. And five, he had to admit it, himself. The Frank Short–Franco Corti war.

He was early; the Squad Office still deserted. A chance to look to his defences. On one of the typists' chairs he found a long dark hair. That would do.

It was for the bottom left-hand drawer of his desk, which he hardly ever used. He took out the drawer above, found some adhesive, stuck one end of the hair to the back of the bottom drawer and the other to the carcass of the desk. It was invisible in the shadow; they'd never spot it, but if they turned the desk over, they'd open that drawer and it would break.

So much for the rubber-heel department. At least he'd done something, though they didn't have to go through his desk or could have done so already. There was nothing for them if they did. Nothing anywhere really. The Fra Angelico was no secret, nor was the money.

Could they have missed the fact he was his father's son? Surely not. The first thing they would do would be to check his record sheet, and it would stare them in the face.

As for the other battles, Denise. All that lovely info? It went against the grain, it went against everything, but it had to be done. The bitch. The French mini-poodle bitch. He laughed out loud, which was remarkable—that long slit mouth rarely so much as smiled. This was one for your Florentine technique, a touch of the Machiavellis. A date for tomorrow. He took a malicious pleasure in ringing her at eight in the morning to get her to the phone in her nightie.

Then Papà. Not a lot he could do on the frighteners front, but on Operation Fifi there was plenty. He rang Sargey Levine.

"Sargey? Listen, I want to talk to the old geezer. If he takes a cab, there's no one lined up to follow, is there?"

"Nah. You'll be all right. Where will you meet him?"

"We used the Science Museum last time."

"Should be okay. Mind you, there's always a bit of a risk anywhere public—never know who you'll bump into do you. 'Ere—did you find out what them coppers' game is, them as is keeping obbo?"

"Yes, I did. Anti-sodding-corruption. They're out of their tiny minds. I mean either they don't know he's my dad or . . . Hold tight. I've thought of something. Could someone be trying to stitch me up? That's it. I bet that's it!" He swore at length, in Italian so as not to give offence. "You've got to keep on your toes these days. Well, leave that one to me. What was I on about? Oh yes, a meeting with the old guv'nor."

"Bring him to my place if you like, you can have the lounge to yourselves. I'll fix a cab, driver as can keep his mouth shut. . . ."

"You're on. After work tonight? I can't keep doing this in the firm's time."

"Yuh. About six, half past then?"

"Right. See you, Sargey."

"See you, boy. Keep dancing."

Keep dancing. That took you back. The school gym, the smell of embrocation, sweat, leather and varnished wood, while you sparred with Sargey. "Come on, boy, keep dancing. Dance and weave. Keep those feet going. On your *toes*, boy! Lord 'elp us, anyone'd fink you was in army boots wiv lead 'eels on em! . . ."

Keep dancing. Keep weaving. Sound advice.

A stitch-up? Is that really it? Now who'd do a thing like that? You've got enemies; you're a copper, dammit, of course you've got enemies. So's all of us. So why you? Who is it feels like that about you? Who, for God's sake? Who hatesya, Baby?

"Right," said Sargey. "I'll have it away. Got everything you want? Make yourselves at home then. Come on, Ma."

Frank Short looked at his father. Six weeks' hair on his head; the tie again, the linen jacket in need of cleaning, but still the grey, unhealthy skin, the nose like a rotten strawberry, the moist currant eyes that never quite met your own.

"Papà, there is a slightly delicate thing which concerns us both."

A complicated look, sly, amused, defensive, a little embarrassed, exceedingly alert. "Is there, son?"

"The thing of a certain lady; perhaps you can guess . . ."

"Do you want me to? I can, but I might guess wrong." (Doing some dancing and weaving of his own.)

"Madame Verdier, Papà . . ."

"Oho! My son is jealous of me! Ah, Franchino, you should remember the English saying: Let the best man win, eh?"

He nearly said something very rude indeed but checked himself in time. *All'Italiana*, this one, *alla Machiavelli*. Old Nonno, who believed in perfidious Albion, would have called it *all'Inglese*. "You have won already, Papà? I congratulate you. And how do you find her? She is good—well, let's put it bluntly—in bed?" (Jab to the solar plexus.)

"Is that a thing a son should say to his father? Has the lady no honour that you should say this?" (Leading with his chin.)

"Not much, Papà. I think she's terrific myself. In bed, I mean. Knows it all, doesn't she? It's a funny sensation, don't you think, making love to a little thing like that. And how she loves it! *Oaoaoah!* Can't get enough of it, can she? Or is that only with a younger man?" (Foul blow, really, below the belt.)

A paroxysm of coughs before the old man stood up, unsteady, holding on to his chair. Frank Short could not bear to see his face and lowered his eyes.

"I shouldn't marry a woman like that if I were you. Because that's what she'll be after. A rich husband with a bad cough; one she can wear out nice and quick!"

His father sat down again and busied himself soaking a filthy handkerchief with spit.

"Oh, and one more thing. Don't tell her anything you wouldn't tell me. She's not very discreet, and she collects insurance rewards." (Right cross to the jaw.)

"Franco! What are you saying? She told you . . . ?"

"Watford, Papà, and Dulwich. If she doesn't get hurt—if, Papà—those should net her twenty or thirty grand. *Capisci?*" (. . . nine, ten, out!)

Cruel to be kind? Not kind to himself, because cutting off his source really hurt. The Doris could risk her own neck but not his father's. And to stop her you had to go for both of them. So he'd done it, though plenty wouldn't.

In theory he could simply have stopped acting on her information; in practice he wouldn't have it in him. Besides, she wouldn't get her money and she'd want to know why, and if it ever got known that Frank Short suppressed information . . . No; this was the only way to play it. And with the Machiavellian spin-off of protecting his children's inheritance. So whatever you've done for the law, Franco boy, you've done a great job for the family, and don't you forget it.

Had he needed to be that brutal? Trouble was, when people shuffled their feet like that, it got on his wick, and his temper these days . . . But you had to put them down. Like in the ring: Once you'd hurt them the dancing slowed and they had to slug it out. Perhaps in this sort of fight as well he was best close in. Strong as a bull but no reach. A quiet bull, a friendly Russian, an unloaded gun.

Time to pick up the bits.

It was all very emotional and Italian; tears, embraces, protestations. It took time, but the old man came as near as he ever would to admitting he'd been infatuated, there had been talk of marriage, he had shown off by talking out of turn.

Silly bitch. Sticking her neck out in front of villains like Blamey. Ought to have known. Perhaps she did, but decided to risk it; those rewards must be life and death for her. She'd certainly gone for the big time. Whatever else Mademoiselle Fifi was, she was game.

"So what will you do, Papà? Stop seeing her?"

A shrug, a spreading of the hands, the reddened, lost-dog eyes all hopeless. "I don't know, son. I suppose I should, but . . . She is stronger than I am, Franco. I just don't know."

"It would be safest, it really would."

A sniff. "And you?"

"I must speak to her, Papà, as I have spoken to you. And I should be present when she is given the insurance rewards. After that, well . . . *Dio mio*, Papà, I am as bad as you. . . ."

Operation Fifi, phase one concluded.

But there was another matter. "Papà, we have told the truth to each other as son to father, as father to son. Now will you tell me this? The Bandenere Botticelli, the Piero di Cosimo *Diana*. You don't want to change—to add anything to what you said before?"

"No, son. I do not. I will swear any oath you like, I will swear away all I possess, but I did not touch those pictures."

No ducking and weaving, nothing combative at all. Could you really believe the old codger when he spoke like that? Hm.

"And the Corti Fra Angelico, Papà?"

"I have told you. I cleaned it, restored only where there was damage, and gave it a coat of mastic. On my life, Franco, that is all."

"And any doubts while you were working on it? I mean it's right, isn't it?"

A flicker? A beginning of a hesitation? "It is right. I am sure it is. There is no one who could have done that, no one. It *must* be quattrocento, and if so, the style . . . Workshop of Fra Angelico without a doubt, and if Willison says the *maestro* . . . He knows, son, better than any of us. That picture is right."

It was after nine when he got home. The air had gone close and stagnant and big cloudbanks hid the sunset; he was sweating after ten yards on his feet. Thunder grumbled a long way off.

Teresa was in the front garden, waiting. Instead of returning his wave, she ran out and clutched him to her. "Oh, Franco! . . ."

"What is it, darling? I said I would be late. . . ."

She answered in Italian—she'd been so good about talking English since they'd left Beak Street. "Franco! A disaster! Your picture, your little *Annunciation* . . ." Sobs. An awful empty ache; the pavement unstable. He lifted her head very gently, not thinking or caring about the neighbours. "Tell me, darling?"

"It's gone! Stolen! I didn't know where to get you. . . ."

He put an arm round her and led her through the first huge scattered raindrops to the gate, up the little paved path between the struggling floribundas and into the house, and suddenly it was she who was the stronger, calling him her baby with his face to her breast, while outside, the sky fell.

CHAPTER 11

WHO HATESYA, BABY?

Indigestion plagued him all night; he awoke with a headache on a Turkish bath of a morning with thunder still around; he missed his exercises and his walk and reached the Yard ten minutes late, running on paracetamol, indigestion pills, and heart capsules.

First the Guv, with shining morning face, shining white collar, stripy shirtsleeves, and Yorkshire Cricket tie. "Morning, Shorty. Take a seat. Well?" You could smell the carbolic across the desk.

"Trouble, Guv. My picture's been nicked—the Fra Angelico."

"Oh aye? Well, don't blame me, lad; I said to put the bugger in the bank, didn't I? Any leads? How'd it happen?"

He told him what he could; the house had been empty from midday till around seven, when Teresa had got back. The ancient Yale on the front door had been slipped, and that was it. Nothing else disturbed, no prints as far as he could tell. No Fra Angelico.

"I tell you, Guv, I wept. I bleeding wept. I mean of all the stupid twits! 'Course I should have had it in the bank, at any rate till the place was made a bit secure and some insurance sorted out. . . ."

"Aye, you should. Well, no use crying over spilt milk; you've reported it locally, have you?"

He nodded. "I got them to mark it *Not for Press.*"

"They'll be forced to call in A & A. I'd not wait for that, lad. I'd get detecting."

"Right, Guv. Thanks."

No word about CIB2. Did he know? Probably not at this stage.

Get detecting. Hm. Legwork, routine enquiries, details for circulation. He briefed Jackie Billings, who was formal and official till he had done, then suddenly a woman. "Oh, I *am* sorry, Mr. Short, and on top of everything else . . ."

"Everything else?"

She put a hand to her mouth. "Oh, gosh! Perhaps I shouldn't have said . . . Look, can Keithy come in a moment?"

The two swapped embarrassed glances. "Go on, Keithy. You tell him. About—you know . . ."

"Yes. Well . . . Well, really it's just . . . Well, these rumours and that. Well, we just wanted to tell you, guv, we don't believe a word of it, and anything we can do . . ."

"We think it's rotten, don't we, Keithy?" A vigorous nod. "Absolutely rotten."

"Thanks. But you might tell me what this is about."

The hand to the mouth again and a little squeak. "Oh! We thought you were sure to know. Well, it's the rubber-heel mob, isn't it? Everyone seems to think . . ."

So the grapevine was on to it; did that include the Guv? Not necessarily. He wanted to hug her. Both of them.

Instead, he nodded gravely. "Thanks, Jackie. I was beginning to wonder, actually . . . Thanks, both of you. It's nice to know who your friends are."

But life had to go on. Frank Short, his coat over his arm, was striding up the hill from the tube towards Whitestone Pond. He was full of an early, hurried lunch and the high sun pounded his back, but the walk was doing him good. He was going to meet a character called Ernie, who had a fixation that the safest place for grassing was among the thickets and copses near the western edge of Hampstead Heath, and the safest time was one o'clock on a Saturday.

Frank Short liked Hampstead. The air was fresher on the hill, and you felt people took art and that for granted instead of running scared like most of the English and leaving it to the women or to queers, foreigners, and cranks.

There were one or two galleries in the street; he stopped to look in a window. Twentieth-century stuff out trad, some decent watercolour landscapes, a drawing or two. There was one that was really good: a copy of something Renaissance? A half-draped woman drawn in red chalk, very sure and delicate and small. He was a few minutes ahead of time and the place was open, so he went in and enquired.

"Yes, it's nice, isn't it? I'll get it out of the window." Typical small-time dealer in T-shirt and sandals.

It *was* nice; really beautifully drawn. At first sight you'd think it was the real thing, only the paper was ordinary cartridge. Initials GS and something else, in a lovely free italic that could have been quattrocento itself—GS for PdC, 1951.

If you had asked Frank Short, he might have agreed that something was going on in the back of his mind, only he hadn't really noticed till you spoke. But no one did, so all he felt consciously was that the drawing mattered.

"Whose is it?" he asked.

"Dunno. A guy brought it in; I think he said some fellow student had done it at art school. I didn't think to ask; or if I did, I've forgotten."

"Any idea who?—I mean the one you got it from?"

"No. I never asked the name."

"Could you describe him?"

"Sorry—you know how it is; it was two or three years ago, and there's so many of them . . . I'd only be guessing."

Frank nodded. "How much d'you want for it?"

A shrug. "Twenty-five? Unframed, that is. I'll be glad to get rid of it, actually." The guy was no salesman.

"Make it twenty then. Cash."

"Okay."

He pressed on, carrying the drawing in a large envelope, up the steep, narrow pavement, past the pond and its snarling model power-boats, to head left-handed into a maze of spinneys.

The meeting, under the usual silver birch, was unproductive. A possible line on some cameos nicked from Solihull Antiques Fair —hardly A & A business; a hint that one Dawkes was up to something—but when wasn't he?—and that was about all. Not worth a fiver really, but it was a nice day, so Frank Short gave him two.

"Why, thanks, guv. Old Bill in the money then?"

"Look on it as a retainer, Ernie. Right?"

" 'Ere, guv. Something else. That Scouse, you want to watch out."

"Oh?"

"Bloody wild, he is, after you sussed his gaff. Mate of Skelton's too, isn't he—him as was nicked in Watford. Know what, guv, he reckons someone blew the bloody whistle. Don't know who, though, does he? But what I says is Gawd 'elp anyone as done it if he finds out; I wouldn't give you that for his chances. . . ." Two fingers jabbed upwards. "So if you should happen to know something about this, you'll know who you got to look arter, won't you? Right, guv?"

"Thanks, Ernie. I won't forget that. Here . . ."

"Blimey! You're a toff, guv. Thanks. That Scouse, he's a bloody maniac; he could get it into his head as it was Gawd knows who. Don't have to get it right, does he?"

"Any idea where he is?"

"Tell you if I did, wouldn't I? I mean the lot of us stands to be clobbered with a daft bloody Mick like that on the loose. . . ."

He returned, thinking hard, clutching his drawing in its envelope, marching across the turf towards the pond. It was scorching on the asphalt surround; he bought himself an ice-cream at a stall. A little to one side, kids and a few parents had gathered round a tent going up or something. He strolled over, licking his ice-cream. It wasn't a tent but a booth. The Punch-and-Judy man! His mind flipped to the Pincio Gardens, a heat that made today's seem gentle, the sun blazing over distant St. Peter's. The crowding, polyglot kids; the balloons, the bubble-gum, the Cokes . . . and a weariness from two sleepless nights on the trot. Must be the fatigue implanted it so deep. . . .

And in the white booth, Pulcinello, a white-clad Mr. Punch with Punch's own voice: belting his Pulcinella, clobbering the *poliziotto*, wheezing into operatic song. And when he'd got home to that monumental bust-up with Teresa, it was Pulcinello and Pulcinella over again. . . .

And now Punch and Judy. He wanted to cry. But inside his head Punch wasn't slugging it out with Judy but with Pulcinello. Punch and Pulcinello and Shorty the policeman. How stupid! Punch *was* Pulcinello; Frank Short *was* Franco Corti. Why, for pity's sake, couldn't they admit it and shut up? He put in a pound note when the hat came round, and in the tube to Charing Cross he was so full of thoughts he nearly missed his station.

That evening Denise came. All right, she was a scrubber, a Doris, a bitch; she was fouling up his life and risking his father's, but he was still hooked. So enjoy it like a good Machiavellian. Pleasure before business for a change. He gave her Asti laced with grappa, and when the bottle was empty he moved in.

Afterwards, he was ashamed. He'd never let himself go like that before, or with such a head of emotional steam. In male-chauvinist mythology she'd have adored it. The reality was different.

". . . *Oaoaoah! Ah! Merde alors!* . . ." More French. It didn't sound ladylike. "You hurt me, Frank . . ."

"*Tant pis* to you, honeybunch."

No, he wasn't proud of himself, but, the steam-pressure was down.

"But why, Frank, why? You who were always so careful with your strength?"

"All right. I'll tell you. At least I'll ask you a question. What are you trying to do to my father?"

"*Oaoaoah!* So *that's* what it is! Well, Frank, your father is a very nice man; he is lonely, he needs a woman to make him care for himself, to clean his house for him. So we are friends. I see him; I do not try to hide it. But that you should be jealous of that . . . *Oah*, Frank! *C'est ridicule!*"

"So you don't . . . ?"

"*Quoi?* You mean . . . ? *Oah, mais non!*"

"And the marrying bit?"

That jolted her. Just when she was getting back into the game.

"Marriage? But that's not true! What is it that makes you think . . . ?"

"Come on, darling, be your age. Smart, attractive woman with your track record; sick old man worth Lord knows what. Stands to reason, doesn't it?" She could play guessing games about how much his father had told him.

"And this is the sort of woman that you think I am? Well then, goodbye!" Great, apart from his fourteen stone on top of her.

"I know exactly what sort you are. You told me."

Silence. Her body twitched under him. Once; twice; then steadily every few seconds. Something told him it wasn't put on.

Soft, wasn't he? A woman only had to cry and he turned to jelly. Your tough, seen-it-all copper. Seconds later they were at it again.

This time it was her turn to play rough. She bit. He winced and let her, obeying some Frank-Shortish sense of justice. One round each.

"Frank, my darrleeng, I have another little secret. . . ."

"Keep it to yourself then."

"*Comment? Mais . . .*"

"Listen, darling; you don't know what you're messing about with, do you? Not a bleeding clue. But Papà knows, and that's one reason he doesn't tell me a thing. Never has done. Doesn't want his face bashed in, does he? And I'm warning you, every time you worm something out of him and pass it on, you bring that one step closer. Not just for him, darling. For you."

"Then why do you tell them? I bring you news; it is for you to decide to use it. . . ."

"Withhold information? You don't know much about policemen. Okay, so preventing crime comes first. But not like that. If the price of catching some miserable thief is murder—that's right, love, murder—then who wants him caught, eh?"

"Murder? What? You mean . . . ?"

"That's right, darling. You, Papà, both of you. That Scouse you shopped last week. Didn't capture him, did we? And he's Liverpool bloody Irish and psychopathic, I shouldn't wonder. He's out for blood, love, and I know that for a fact. Okay, he may be thick, but once he puts two and two together . . . You know my father had a warning? After the Watford caper. So here's this poor old git daren't open his bleeding mouth, and you have to take a jemmy to it and bring me the results. They'll suss you sure as eggs, if they haven't done already, and God help you when they do. Now do you get the message?"

She nodded and sat up, swivelling to face him, with the eyes of a woman of sixty. No more crying, no more nonsense, no more hope.

Operation Fifi complete.

Dressed and ready to go, she laughed, more to herself than him.

"*Adieu, petit piaf!*"

"Come again?"

"*Piaf.* You remember Edith Piaf?"

"Yes."

"It was not her name, you know; she took it. You know what that means, *piaf?*"

He shook his head.

"Sparrow, the slang for sparrow. It is for that I chose *Spadger*; Piaf and I, we were not so different; the little sparrows that peck in the gutter and the cats eat them. So goodbye, *piaf*, goodbye, Spadger—that's all." *Très français, n'est-ce pas?* Poor little bitch. Spadger. Cats' meat.

Next morning he checked his desk. The hair was broken. Now what? Things were that hair-trigger (joke?) these days; a breath in someone's ear, the merest whisper of suss, and out. Back in uniform, sorting out traffic jams in darkest Neasden, and that was if you were lucky. Or suspended, to bite your nails and go sour while they made their minds up. It had happened so often, and to men he *knew* weren't bent. The things a few rotten apples could do . . .

And there was nothing at all he could do about it. It couldn't be just his father. It would be sad but understandable if they said, "Sorry, mate, you can't go on in A & A now you're on speaking terms with your old guv'nor, what with him being in the trade and that." But if that was all, then why the secrecy and the snooping? It *had* to be someone fitting him up. Who? Who hates you that much?

Around six that evening on his way to Green Park tube, he was waiting to cross the Mall when a car pulled in. For a moment he didn't recognize it, then the near door opened and a figure leaned across. "Hello, Frank. Like a lift home?"

The Silverman Workwagon and his receptionist, Fiona. Fiona Rat——? Rat-race? Rattray. Nice kid. She'd blown him a kiss once.

"Why, Fiona! That's nice of you. Yes, please."

When he was settled he asked, "How's the gallery? Happy in your work?"

"Not very."

"I'm sorry. Any special reason?"

"Not really. Except—oh, I just don't hit it off with Mr. Silverman."

"Oh?" He turned his head. He liked her in profile: small features, a firm little chin, the thick dark brows frowning as if she'd been having a row. "What's wrong with him?"

"Oh, I don't know. He's always so high and mighty, so *smooth*. You feel you're being condescended to; treated as—not just an employee, a *servant*. Oh, a very superior one, but still a slave. As if he goes through the motions but actually he doesn't give a damn. Sometimes I think he hates me . . . for being . . . well, you know—I mean from my sort of background." Her voice had lost that maddening too-too-county ring for the classlessness of educated youth. "It's not that he's unkind or inconsiderate or anything. Oh, perhaps it's just me, but . . ."

"Yes?"

"But—perhaps I oughtn't to say this, specially with you being a policeman, but . . . Look, you mustn't take this the wrong way because I haven't really anything to go on—but sometimes I do wonder whether he's quite—well, honest if you like."

"It's a funny game, the art trade. What's straight, what's bent, it's not always that clear, is it? Still, I'm glad you've told me. And if anything does come up, you can give me a ring. How d'you get on with his wife?"

"All right. She doesn't really work at the gallery; just stands in now and then. I quite like her, actually."

Toffee-nosed bint like this liking that old harpy? You never could tell. "Good. I'm glad to hear it."

"Well, she is what she is. You know—common as muck and doesn't try to hide it, not really. But with him . . . Always being the country gentleman or something, know what I mean?"

He did. The only genuine thing he'd seen in Silverman was his delight when his wife turned up that time. And one other, less endearing thing—that second of recognition when those unrevealing eyes were suddenly hostile.

Who hatesya, Baby? Silverman? Why not?

CHAPTER 12

BODILY HARM

He didn't ask her in. She looked at him a bit starry-eyed, he thought, when he thanked her and said good night; those clear, light-blue eyes were starry enough anyway with their naturally dark lashes. He half wondered if she fancied him, but that was silly; a classy girl like that, a real lady, she'd be going round with Guards officers, lords, rich young bankers—what would a girl like that want with a middle-aged, raddie copper? Nice kid, though, and worth cultivating, because a friend at the Silverman Gallery who disliked the boss could be very handy indeed.

GS for PdC. Piero di Cosimo? Why not? He had no mental image of a Piero di Cosimo drawing, so he had nothing in his mind to compare with the GS one, but the style wouldn't be far off. The first thing he did at work next morning was get out the photographs of the *Diana and Actaeon*.

If he'd hoped his drawing would reveal itself as the sketch for one of the forest nymphs, he was disappointed, but it seemed to belong. It was hard to believe that *PdC* in that sensitive Renaissance hand could be anything but that. *GS for PdC: for*, not *after*. A tingle of excitement crept through him. Not so much because it was a lead in a sizeable case, but because if GS was the culprit, then AC, namely Antonio Corti, wasn't.

He summoned Keith Billings, who he was beginning to discover had tenacity, a head for detail, and a visual memory worth respect. How he'd disliked that man at first! And the Guv had agreed he was useless. But once Keith'd settled down and especially since his marriage, he had become quite an asset. And now that he was more secure, he was beginning to come across—in spite or perhaps because of that olive-eyed, red-and-cream face with a moustache like two anchovies on a pizza—as something of a "man of trust."

"GS, Keith, 1951. He's likely to be British, or English-speaking, writing *for* like that. So what I want from you is a list of all the GSs in the business old enough to have been around in 1951—maybe as students. Try *Who's Who in Art* and Benezit."

"Okey-dokey. Any special time factor?"

"Not really. Only don't hang about, this is big stuff. And, Keith—keep an eye skinned for a calligrapher."

"Will do. Can I take the drawing? Someone might recognize the style."

"I'd rather hang on to it. Get it photographed if you like."

"I can do that myself."

"I didn't know you were a photographer."

"Well, I'm not exactly Cecil Beaton, but I take an interest. Matter of fact—you remember Blamey's place in Dulwich?"

"I didn't go there myself."

"I took a few shots. You know—for the Billings Archive. Besides, he'd got all kinds of stuff in there; so I says to myself, you never know, a record might come in handy. It just struck me, you might care to take a butcher's. I'll bring them in some time if you like."

"Yes. Do that. That's it, then? Off you go."

Now then, the Fra Angelico. It was too early to expect results, but meanwhile there was a job he'd like to do, and now that there was a theft to investigate, he could do it in the firm's time and draw expenses.

He had got the address from his father, who was horrified when he rang him with the news and did a lot of brassy coughing before he could say two words in succession: the Honourable Lavinia Perry, widow or divorced, South Lodge, Frattisham, Norfolk. He had rung to make an appointment and been offered lunch. He had got permission to use his car and had brought it to work. It was time to go if he wasn't going to be late.

That picture was a puzzle. Right as rain, they all said, but his father said it as if he had needed convincing, or perhaps his head, once convinced, had overruled his instinct. Frank Short was sure he hadn't been lying; the picture had been in good shape, he'd done a minimum of work on it, well and conscientiously, *but* . . .

So he was going to see this lady in Norfolk.

He hadn't bargained on an Honourable—the lady in her cottage who had been overjoyed to get two thousand had suggested a retired village postmistress or something. But a lord's daughter! He'd put on his new best suit, gloating for a moment over the *By Appointment* on the name-tag, and over the comfort, because as a rule nothing ever fitted him. A real toff's suit, dark grey and discreetly pin-striped, though not so dark as Franco Corti's invariable near-black. And with it, one of his silk ties from Cousin Matteo's *merceria* in Florence, which he hadn't felt like wearing since the heart attack, because Frank Short (still a fantasy at that time) wouldn't be seen dead in them. A fine flamboyant tie with great swirls of white and blue and a dash of magenta. No doubt about it, somewhere inside him Franco Corti was staging a comeback. Just as well. He'd be better company at lunch than Frank Short.

Frattisham was in flat, bare country punctuated with mournful Russian-looking pinewoods. Bleak after hot old London, with a crosswind from the north-east and a white sky. A huddle round a grand perpendicular church, a factory farm, council houses, then tremendous park gates in an endless wall, and, leading through them to nowhere visible, a potholed track with electric cattle-fencing on the right, and on the left South Lodge.

It was stone-built, small and Gothic-baronial. It had roses round the door (they had black spot and needed dead-heading), a scraggy little lawn, a muddle of flowers, vegetables, and weeds. A motley rabble of dogs shot out, barking hysterically. He stayed in the car.

A voice screamed, "Chumley! Pooh! Buggins! Get back inside!" The barks got louder, and the Honourable Lavinia Perry came round the corner of the house. "Mr. Short? Sorry about Buggins, he'll calm down in a minute. Gentle as a lamb. *Do* come in. Shut up, damn you! Not you, Mr. Short . . ."

She was middle-aged, lumpy of face and figure, with brown, well-looked-after hair; dressed in disgraceful old slacks, a ditto cardigan with one button taking all the strain, and about twenty thousand pounds' worth of diamond ring.

Inside, it was beautiful; the sitting room all flowers and Meissen and Hepplewhite, plus a stunning little grandmother clock. Two Georgian racehorse pictures. A portrait of a smiling girl that had to be Romney.

"Drink, Mr. Short? Whisky and soda? Dubonnet? Gin? I shouldn't advise the sherry; it's been open since Easter."

He settled for Dubonnet as the least unsuitable—he loathed gin, and whisky was for crises. She gave him about a quarter-pint of it, without ice, in a delicate engraved wineglass, and poured herself a giant whisky that she drowned in soda. "Happy days. Did you have a good journey?"

Lukewarm Dubonnet was not his drink. He sipped it from politeness while his hostess downed her whisky and another like it and made extended conversation till lunch.

Smoked salmon ("Henry goes up for the whole of February and catches them in shoals"), casserole of deep-freeze pheasant. Claret. "Oh, do. Henry says it wants drinking. (Henry was her titled brother up at the Hall.) No, not for me; I'll stick to whisky and soda."

The claret was out of this world; it was only after the third glass he plucked up courage to ask, " 'Scuse me, Mrs. Perry" (not madam or anything; he'd checked with Bob Wellow, whose father had been a gentleman's gamekeeper), "would you think it rude if I asked what I'm drinking?"

"That? Oh, it's something Grandpa laid down after the war. Rothschild? Is there a Château Rothschild? Never touch it meself. . . ."

Over coffee among the Hepplewhite, with apologies for the absence of port, she let him get down to work.

"This painting you sold to Mr. Corti. It's been stolen, and I wondered if you could tell me anything of its history."

Eyebrows went up. "Stolen? Well, blow me down! Yes, I can tell you a little. It was given to me, actually, just after I got married."

"Oh yes?"

"Of course Anni always pretended it was a Fra Angelico, but that was poppycock."

"Annie?"

"It was on our honeymoon; it was supposed to be a sort of consolation prize, only back to front." Her eyes were many years away.

"I'm sorry, Mrs. Perry, I'm not quite with you."

Was there a hint of impatience? As if anyone but a clown would have known. "Jack and I were honeymooning in Monte, and Anni gave it to me, and whatever anyone else says, I think it was a damned sporting thing to do."

"Sorry, Mrs. Perry. Annie who?"

The eyes returned to the present. They were brown and rather cowlike. "How stupid of me; one's so apt to think everyone knew Anni. Annibale Bandenere. Jack beat him by a short head, you see."

"Count Bandenere? No, I hadn't heard of that one."

"Oh, a charmer, an absolute charmer, and rich as Croesus. Terribly naughty, of course . . ."

"He wouldn't be related to Count Eugenio delle Bandenere, would he?"

"Eugenio? Oh yes, that's his boy. Haven't seen him since he left Harrow, which I blush to say he did rather hastily." Her voice went confidential. "You see, he was known as *Janey*. Still is. Oh dear, I'm getting talkative in my cups. Goodness, I never offered you any brandy."

"No, thanks; it's kind of you, but I've a long drive. Tell me, when you sold the painting, was it you or Mr. Corti who made the first approach?"

"I'll tell you what happened. You see, the dry-rot got into my attic and Henry was being stingy, so I asked Silverman (Henry *invests* in art, he usually buys through Silverman; says he's the most *frightful* scoundrel, but better the devil, you know) I asked him would he be interested in the picture. It never really went with my other things, and now that Anni's dead, and . . . Well, *something* had to go. Anyway, Silverman said he thought he knew the picture and would I bring it in when I was in town . . . and before you could say 'Jack Robinson,' this *sweet* little man appears on the doorstep and offers two thousand then and there, in *notes*, if you please . . . and honestly, I was so glad to have the whole thing settled and off my mind . . . I mean what's money anyway? So I let him have it. Silverman was awfully cross. Serve him jolly well right, say I, if he can't be bothered to get off his fat bottom."

"Fair enough. This is really helpful. Can I ask you one last thing, and then I must be off—you didn't believe Count Bandenere when he said it was a Fra Angelico. Might I ask why?"

"For two very good reasons. One, he was *the* most awful liar; and two, well, he may have been extravagant and he loved to make a gesture, and very handsome it was, but would *you* go giving Fra Angelicos to a gal who's just given you the push?"

He was glad to be away and heading for London; he never felt at ease in the country, and the drive was a chance to think.

Shouldn't have drunk so much. His blood-alcohol must be over the limit. He drove extra carefully, feeling headachy and overfed. Bitter too, because, stolen or not, if his lovely *Annunciation* was wrong . . . He growled and let the growl crescendo to a bull-roar of frustration.

Bandenere, Silverman—the two names linked again. With one dodgy picture, so what? With two, suspicious; with three, knocking on conclusive. That GS again; it had to be. What an artist, to fool Gervase Willison.

Or had he? It could still be coincidence; Anni Bandenere could have been that quixotic, or stoned, or uncaring; or just mistaken; he could have thought the picture was wrong when it was right all the time.

Grrrrr!

Prrp, prrp, said the phone. "Chief Inspector Short? One moment, please; Commander Thomas wishes to speak to you."

For a moment he panicked. Thomas? Who was Thomas? CIB2? The end? Disgrace, disaster . . . ?

"Is that Short? Thomas, Commissioner's office. I've an envelope for your friend Spadger." *For this relief much thanks.* Shakespeare.

He set it up for the same evening in the Friends' room at the Gibbonsian (they'd made him an honorary Friend of Grinling Gibbons after the Tondo caper), which was hardly the sort of place where you'd run into your Blameys and that, and when Informant Spadger had said could she take him out for a meal to celebrate and have coffee afterwards at his place, he'd weakened and said yes, only she mustn't pay for him or there'd be trouble.

The room was open till six-thirty; they were to meet there at six fifteen. He'd put on his posh suit for the occasion, with a black Franco Corti hat, and arrived, simultaneously with Commander Thomas, ten minutes early. Apart from Denise being ten minutes late, it went swimmingly; Thomas gave her a fat envelope, she counted the money in the Ladies' and signed *Spadger* on the receipt, according to the rules.

"That's it then," said Thomas. "It's been a pleasure, madam. Good night."

This was Denise's evening, so they were going to eat French and really well. It was early to start drinking. They could have gone to Balfour Road for a quick piece of your action-packed but they didn't fancy the journey. So, as it was a lovely, sunny evening, they decided on St. James's Park.

He wasn't happy about that; they could be seen too easily and the word passed on to Teresa—or, more dangerously, to your Blameys and that. It was the little-finger syndrome again; she was impossible to refuse. Operation Fifi had been different, but that was Spadger the grass, not Denise the woman. So was this, really, but . . . *Che sarà, sarà.* Lie back and enjoy it.

"How much was it?" he asked as they leant over the bridge.

"So *much*, Frank! Twenty-three thousand pounds! Twenty-three thousand! I have never had such money before. Oh, I want to *spend* it, *all* of it. No, no, I shan't, not all; perhaps I must live on that for a long time. But perhaps not, so I shall enjoy myself a little. Help me, Frank. Help me to enjoy myself."

What she was really saying, he thought, was what was the point in saving for a life that might end tomorrow? In which case, what was the point of saving?

Answer: Life didn't have to be cut short. And for the kids, families, dependents. Who depended on Denise? Frank Short, a bit; Antonio Corti, a bit, but emotionally, not financially. No; no dependents.

The hand in the end of the arm that was round her kept edging to her breast. He let it; so did she. In public? Why not? This was the eighties.

"Denise?"

"Yes?"

"You really fancy me, don't you?"

"But of course. You are a formidable lover and a very attractive man. And *solide, hein?* A man even a woman can trust . . ."

"Like Teresa?"

"*Oah non!* Not the trust of a wife; the trust of a mistress. It is not the same thing. What harm does it do to her if we make love?" Instinctively they were walking now towards the shrubberies. Round the second turn, behind a laurel, he stopped and kissed her. How this woman turned him on!

"*Oaoaoah!* Careful, Frank—*ah, non!* Come on, let us walk some more. . . ."

It was there that it happened, as they turned back side by side towards the open park. His reflexes had him moving before he knew why. He hurled her into a holly bush and ducked. He brought up an arm to spoil the aim. Something splashed his neck. Arm-lock now, and a knee . . .

The man groaned and crumpled and Frank Short was on him, pinning him down half-strangled, while Denise thrashed about screaming and throat-scarring chemical fumes rose in his face.

"Denise! Shut up! Are you all right?"

"*Non! Oah!* What is this? It hurts me, Frank—what *is* it?"

"Vitriol! Wash it off quick—is there much on you?"

"No, no, a drop. Ah! *Merde!* That really hurts!"

"Well, wash it off *quick*, woman, for Christ's sake! The lake! Go on, *run!*"

His neck was hurting a lot now; it was only a small patch, thank heaven, and a few scattered drops, but those fumes . . . He was starting to cough. Where were they coming from?

He looked down. His beautiful new jacket was reeking under his nose.

CHAPTER 13

OUT

There is a way of taking a man where he doesn't want to go by walking beside him with his arm through yours like a shotgun over a sportsman's. You brace his elbow across your forearm and a touch stops any nonsense with his free hand. He'll come.

Frank Short used this grip to take his man to the waterside, where he managed with Denise's help to get his coat off and wash the acid from his neck. The coat had had it. With an end-of-an-era feeling and an emperor's gesture, he threw it in the lake.

Denise was in a mess. The ethnic blouse was spattered, with some drops on her face and the worst mercifully over her bra, which had given some protection. It was weird how little notice people took. The one old lady who offered help looked as if she needed it more than they did. Otherwise, they might have been walking the dog.

It was more than half a mile to the nearest nick, across Victoria Street in Rochester Row. He didn't want Denise there at first because of the gossip, but she needed first aid and something to wear; meanwhile the wet, ruined blouse had to do. He handed in his goon like a piece of luggage—he'd hardly so much as looked at him, found a WPC to attend to Denise, and was free to think about the damage.

The pain was fierce; Denise was pale and swimmy-eyed, lips pressed together, catching her breath every few seconds. Her face was hardly marked, but her chest and shoulder would have coin-sized scars. As for himself, there was a three-inch burn on his neck and a spatter on the jaw. Their eyes, mercifully, were untouched. His coat had taken the worst. A hero's death.

When Denise was patched up, he sent her home, under pro-test, because she still hankered for that dinner. Business before pleasure, he told her, and went down to question his man.

Arthur Gudgeon, unemployed lorry driver, Kentish Town. The computer said he had form—car theft, threatening behaviour, GBH. Lorry driver indeed. They ought to introduce a new cate-gory, villain's minder. Gudgeon, like a good professional, stuck to what lawyers call vulgar abuse. Frank Short left him to the locals and went home.

He faced a long, lonely evening, with Teresa at the Trattoria and only the telly and the garden to distract him from his pain. The telly was dismal, he wasn't in a gardening mood and couldn't face the kitchen. He poured himself a Scotch on the rocks and sat over his unread *Telegraph*, mourning his suit.

It was Thursday. The children's half-term would start next eve-ning, and they were coming to Balfour Road for ten days' dummy run before seeing the term out from Beak Street. After that it would be one hundred per cent Acton and West London schools in the autumn. If it weren't for his burns and the loss of his coat; if it weren't for CIB2 and his father—his health, the threats to his safety; if it weren't for himself—his infatuation with Denise, his fear of a heart attack, his Frank Short persona cringing under an Eyetie backlash; if it weren't for all that, he'd really be looking forward to those ten days. As it was . . . He swore vilely and uncharacteristically in Italian and poured another drink to wash down a heart capsule.

It was a relief when the phone rang. He was still thinking in Italian and he answered, "Corti."

"Good evening, Chief Inspector. Am Hector. Have informations. Do you like that I should give them now or shall we meet together?"

Something to think about. "I'll come round. Can you fix me some food?" It was after nine.

"We shall keep something. *Pasta in brodo,* or we have a fine *risotto ai funghi,* then *scaloppine alla . . .*"

"Not now, do you mind? Whatever's going. With you in half an hour. See you."

"*Ciao,* Chief Inspector."

He took the car, which was a maxi, acquired with a determination to buy British and a hope it would take the whole family, which it just about did for short runs. He managed to park not far from the Trattoria, where Hector Dando greeted him like a five-star *maître d'hôtel* and bullied him into ordering excessively before he would let him upstairs to the children.

They were excited and noisy, and old Nonna had called in Teresa as a reinforcement. There was no room to move in the old-fashioned, over-furnished lounge, and it was some moments before he noticed his father. Looking awful, his normally plump face lined and withered, the skin dry, as if a puff of wind would blow him flat. But meanwhile he had to fend off the children and explain to each in turn that the dressing on his neck meant it hurt if you threw your arms round it.

"What did you do to it, Dad?"

"I didn't do anything, it was someone else."

"Who?"

"A man called Gudgeon."

"Is he a villain?"—"Did you get him, Dad?"—"Will he go to prison?"—"What did he do?"—"Why?"—"Was it another fight?"—"Was he trying to escape arrest?"—"Where's your coat?"

"*Hush,* all of you, and I'll tell you. He *is* a villain; he *will* go to jail; he was throwing vitriol at a lady . . ." He could have bitten his tongue off; he felt Teresa's hackles go up.

"*What* lady, Franco?"

"An informant." This time his father's face changed. Good grief, he looked ill. Teresa sniffed and let it be; not for long, he thought, we'll hear more about this.

Gino, he noticed, had stayed quiet. Gino, the eldest, fourteen next month, was as tall as he was and a son to be proud of. His face was impassive till you saw his eyes, dark and open, resting on you in a way that made you feel perhaps you weren't such a disaster after all. "You got vitriol on your new suit?" It was a commiseration rather than a question. Gino knew.

Frank Short turned to his father. "Well, Papà? How goes it?"

The old man looked at him with no courage in his eyes. "I am getting old, Franco." The tinny, brassy voice compelled your attention. "And I have business worries."

Like parcels of grass? "You don't look well, Papà; have you seen a doctor?" A shake of the grey head. "Don't you think you should?"

"What about? When a man is my age" (only sixty-four, dammit!), "he cannot expect to feel always at his best. No, Franco." Heels dug in; a small child saying, *shan't*. For thirty years Antonio Corti had mistrusted doctors; they had let his wife die—or, in his bitterer moments, killed her. It was no use pressing the point. No doctors. Such a frightened little man. No policemen, no surrender, no sense.

"And the business, Papà?"

A shrug. "Nothing you do not know of. But you must tell me about this assault; you say a lady?" He knew who it was all right. "She was harmed?"

"A few drops, mostly the chest and shoulder. I do not think she will dare to bring us any more information—indeed I do not think she will be able to get it now." Poor old man; mind and body, he was really suffering. He put a hand on his shoulder. "Don't worry, Papà, you'll be all right. A year or two and you'll have Gino to help you look after yourself, then Sylvie, and then

Ches. Before you know where you are, you'll have a whole family of strong young grandchildren to support your old age. Look at them, Papà, aren't they lovely? Aren't you proud of them?"

"I shall be sad to lose them; I shall not see much of them when they have gone to Acton. Why do you have to do it, son?" The old man knew the answer; he didn't really want it again. Frank Short felt his shoulders bow physically under the guilt and had to brace himself upright.

Hector Dando broke it up by announcing his dinner—the others, as usual, had eaten before the restaurant opened. He kissed the children one by one, picking up little Gracie and Tony to swing them high in the air, though they were getting rather big for that. "Good night, my sweethearts. See you tomorrow."

"'Night, Dad. See you."

Tomorrow. Great. So why did he feel so tearful about them all?

"The risotto was okay? Not too much oregano? You are sure you would not like more?" You'd think Hector had been in the business all his life instead of six months, and that supposedly book-keeping.

"No, thanks. And not too much of the *scaloppine*, please."

Useless. The portion was twice what the customers got; he ought to leave at least half. But Hector would be desolate and the kitchen insulted, and anyway, it was so darn good. . . . He avoided a second helping with difficulty. By now there was half a litre of the house Chianti inside him—Uncle Paolo's, of course, and excellent, though a little young. Anaesthetic. The world was improving slightly.

"Now then, Hector," he said when the salad was cleared and the fruit bowl on the table. "Sit down—glass of wine? Information; what have you got for me?"

"Count Eugenio delle Bandenere: born Monte Carlo, twenty-seven May 1954 . . ."

He couldn't resist a bit of one-upmanship. "Son of Count Annibale, now dead. Expelled from Harrow, passive homosexual,
known as Janey."

"You know that? You never said it."

"Don't worry, Hector; I only found out yesterday." Was it really that recent?

A grave acknowledging inclination. "They are very rich people.
There are two sisters, married to men richer than their brother;
Count Eugenio has all the money. Has land, two thousand hectares, in Campania. Was three thousand hectares, and some more
near Tivoli, but he sells it. Monte Carlo, the baccarat, especially
the baccarat—and a wife was a starling from Cinecittà . . ."

"Starlet. A starling is a bird."

Out with the notebook. "Excuse?"

Frank Short explained again.

"I get it. These starlets, they cost much. The jewels, the yacht,
the clothes. As well as the baccarat. So Count Eugenio sells every
year more hectares. . . ."

"Married? Is he really the way they say he is?"

"I think he is all the ways. The wife is also for decoration, for
status. And perhaps for countlets? But there are not. No children.
And certain he has his men, a teacher of ski, a German sailor. For
this one a Lotus, for that a Lamborghini . . ."

"And furniture, antiques, paintings?"

"Like the hectares. One nice painting, not special but nice, he
can buy five or six automobiles for his friends."

"The classic scenario, eh?" Did it really exist? "And the law.
Any difficulties?"

"In Monaco, I think no. In Italy, difficulties with taxes, naturally; it is normal."

"So he sells pictures. You don't happen to know what's gone in
the last ten years?"

"Excuse." Out came the notebook. "I asked special about the

pictures. I have the important ones. One Guardi, one Zuccarelli. That is all."

"Are you sure?" Guardi and Zuccarelli were all right if you liked that sort of thing, but not top class. "You're sure there's nothing else? No Botticelli? No Piero di Cosimo?"

"I am certain. My source will not be mistaken."

Now that was really odd.

Friday morning and the in-tray overflowing; his neck and jaw smarting steadily; worries lying doggo while he got on with his work. Bob Wellow processing paper opposite. A knock on the door. The male voice duet, "Come in!"

"Morning, Mr. Wellow." Keith Billings, pizza-faced, with his big pizza grin. "Morning, guv. Your list."

"What list? Oh, the GS names. Thanks."

"Would you like a shufti at these? Château Morrison, Dulwich?"

"Morrison? Oh, Blamey. Thanks, Keith. Chuck them in the basket. That the lot?"

"Yessah! The lot, sah!" Keith Billings threw a big jokey salute and went.

His photographs were on top of the heap. He had been right, there was all sorts of stuff; Blamey alias Morrison fancied his taste. The first print was mostly expensive grot like Chippendale TV sets and life-size china doggies, but there were some nice things too. The pictures on the walls were marquetry—a landscape, a nude of the kind known as saucy. He moved on to the next and exclaimed, "Bloody hell!"

"Eh?" said Bob.

"Sorry. Got a clue, as you might say. A link between Blamey and our Max."

"Max? Oh, Silverman." Bob wasn't interested.

The clue was a portrait over Morrison's fireplace. It had been in Silverman's window last summer, labelled *François Boucher*

1703–1770. A pricey, primped, powdered little Louis XVI Fifi
la Fanny. He heard his father's voice, with the old chuckle
in it and without that new unhealthy timbre, "Who am I
to contradict him, son? *I* don't say Boucher. I don't say anything.
I just do my work."

Ten minutes later he was summoned by the Guv to find Commander Thomas of the Commissioner's staff seated beside him.
They looked at him hard, Thomas po-faced, Papworth the same
but embarrassed, saying, "Sit down, Chief Inspector." Not *Shorty*
but *Chief Inspector*. Trouble.

Thomas did the talking. "Chief Inspector Short, it is my duty
under Section 49 of the Police Act, 1964, to inform you that certain facts have come to light which could lead to criminal
charges. I am obliged to notify you of the nature of these facts
and can best do so by asking you to look at these documents."

The world was yawing on its axis; soon it would fall into the
sun or career into outer space. For a moment he could not focus
on the papers thrust before him.

". . . statement from the Acton branch of the Mayfair and
Marylebone Building Society showing the state of Mr. Frank
Short's account. Mr. Short, of what looked like an accommodation address, was in credit by three thousand pounds plus a little interest. Attached to the account was Mr. Short's application
to open it, bearing Frank Short's own signature dated six weeks
ago on the third of May.

There were also two letters addressed to the branch by one
William Short from an address in Gloucestershire. "I have pleasure in enclosing my son's application form, signed by him, together with the sum of one thousand pounds which you will
kindly place to his credit. . . ." And the next, less than three
weeks old: "Please find enclosed a further two thousand pounds
for credit of the account of my son Frank Short."

"Used notes of mixed denominations," Thomas said, looking
grim. "I understand, Chief Inspector, that Short is not your fa-

ther's name, nor are these letters in his handwriting. Have you anything to say?"

"I have, sir! By God, I have! This is a con, a total fabrication. That signature's forged; I never saw that form in my life, I've never had a building-society account. I don't know that address. Someone's fitting me up, sir . . ."

They let him go on for five minutes, Papworth looking more and more worried, Thomas less and less, till he cut him short.

"Very well, Chief Inspector. Your remarks will be noted and checked. The matter will be investigated further. Meanwhile, you are suspended from duty on full pay. Here is your notification in the required form. Warrant card, if you please."

Punch-drunk, he handed it over, then collected his wits enough to enquire, "Can I ask one question, please? This William Short . . . ?"

"Doesn't exist. I would have thought that was obvious. Nothing else, Chief Inspector? You will of course be given the opportunity to put your case at the proper time."

He shrugged his shoulders in reply.

"All right, you may go. And you may not, repeat not, come back."

CHAPTER 14

DEATH OF AN ENGLISHMAN

It wouldn't hold water. It couldn't. What could they do? Check the accommodation address for a start, see if Frank Short's mail had been collected or forwarded, and get either a description or an address, because the building society would have sent some kind of statement or notification there, surely? And if the mail was still there? Then they'd check with the building society. They'd done that and he'd seen the results. Hm. They mightn't find the holes in it, not that way.

Trouble is, he decided, moping on a park bench, trouble is, they won't want it with holes in, they'll want it sewn up. All right, if it's criminal charges, they've got to make them stick, but if it's just discipline . . . An allegation, the merest whiff of doubt, and I'll be off the Squad and driving a desk in bloody Neasden. So what you have to do, Franco Corti—and stuff Frank Short, because you're fighting for your life and you play this strictly *alla Machiavelli*—what you have to do is give them cast-iron proof it's a fit-up, and hand them whoever did it on a plate. Hung, drawn, stuffed, trussed, roast and ready to carve. Hm.

His first bout of misery was over, and the sensation of going to war was strengthening. War against whom, for pity's sake? Max Silverman? It had to be. Point one, Silverman knew he was after him; he'd known that since last summer, when he'd marched into the gallery got up as a customer for Silverman's private stock and Silverman sussed him and slung him out. Friend Max wouldn't forgive him for that though he was in the clear, peddling his expensive under-the-counter filth with its veneer of artistic merit. Nor would he forgive him for bringing half the Squad to Vee's private view. And it wasn't just not forgiving; it was survival, because as long as Franco Short or Frank Corti or whoever was around, Max Silverman wasn't safe and he knew it. So Maxie had to bust him. So war has been declared. All right, Maxie boy, let's go.

GS for a start. A flank attack, the point being that if GS was the faker, he must have dealings with Silverman. And if he could write GS *for PdC* in that perfect Renaissance script, then why couldn't he write *F. Short* on a building-society form the way F. Short had written it in Silverman's visitors' book? So look for GS. Keith Billings's list was in his pocket. His suspension made no difference, because the three Renaissance paintings, GS, Blamey, the threats to his father, the attack on Denise, and now this salvo against himself were all part of the Corti-Silverman war.

So GS. Forty or fifty names, some familiar, some not. Difficult without the Yard's resources. So? Instinct—a somewhat Italian instinct—said, Go to your friends. Among that generation of English artists his friend, in spite of everything, was Sir Frederick Bugler, PPRG, PPRBS. He went home, collected his drawing, rang Fred Bugler, and arranged to call at the big St. John's Wood house.

After last year's disaster, Sir Fred had talked about moving from the house, but instead he and Vee had given up their flat in the main block and camped in the studio wing, where, wheelchair or no wheelchair, he beat his daughter to the door.

"Franco! How splendid! Haven't seen you for months. You'll stay to lunch? Yes, of course you will. What are you drinking? Hello—what have you been doing to your neck?" Same old hospitable glad-to-see-you Fred; the ginger sideburns white-streaked now and merged into a spectacularly bi-coloured beard, the frizz round the bald pate more grey than sandy, but still the same. Not a man of trust but still a friend, if only because of Vee.

They sat in the makeshift kitchen, and the drinks were down to beer or Cyprus sherry; he took the sherry. Vee surfaced, kissed him and dived back into the studio.

"Well, Franco, what can I do for you?"

"This drawing. It's supposed to have been done by someone who was a student in the early fifties—GS. I wondered if by any wild chance you could . . ."

Fred was looking at it with the same twist-drill penetration Vee's eyes had had while she was doing his portrait.

"Gilbert," he said. "Little Gilbert. That's your man. He was at the Gibby with me. Amazing chap. Runty little beggar, hardly knew how to talk, always hiding away in holes and corners, but he could draw like an angel from heaven. Damned fine painter too, when he ever did any. Never came to anything. . . ."

"Gilbert who, Fred?"

"Oh Lord, I'm terrible about names . . . Smart? Sweeny? . . ."

Frank Short was going down Keith's list: George, Geoffrey, Gertrude, Gordon, Galatea, Gilbert! "Sweet?" he asked.

"That's it. Gilbert Sweet. That's him, I bet you anything you like. Couldn't find a style of his own, you see, always imitating. You'd watch him draw and one day it would be Ingres, the next Michelangelo or Leonardo—only back to front, because of Leonardo being left-handed—and honestly, you couldn't tell the difference. He'd even sign them now and then—he could do all their signatures perfectly.

"And to hear him talk, when he did get going! He'd be on about some drawing by Raphael or someone and it'd be an equal telling you about an equal. He *knew*, Franco. It was uncanny. He won the Hogarth, of course—that was an Italian primitive—tempera, gold leaf, the lot. And then he sunk without trace. Rum world, isn't it?"

He got Fred to ring the Gibbonsian for him, suggesting it was best if the police were kept out of it, and Fred came back with an address, old but at least something. Cowslip Close, Hare Hill, Queensend, Upton on Severn, Worcestershire.

"Fred, you don't know what you've done for me; this is terrific. Gilbert Sweet, Upton on Severn. Right."

Upton on Severn? Fred had a road atlas. Two and a half hours? Not more. He nearly took off then and there, but it was lunch time and Tarleton Hill was therapeutic, so he stayed for bread and cheese and apples. Vee let him help with the washing up, which was more than Teresa ever did, and he wasn't much good at it. Then he left. They'd want to be back at work.

How it had all changed. No wine, no salads. No Denise. Denise? Must phone her. See how she was. Get the action going again. Must he really? The realization that he didn't want to was like coming out of prison.

He found a place for the Maxi in Hyde Park and got out to walk, through moist heavy heat under a thick blue and mauve sky with enormous distant cummuli. Exercise and thought. He headed towards the West End, the centre of the world's art markets, and in a very special way his patch. Its dealers, its sale-rooms, its galleries had been his life. His own possession.

Out.

He growled and found himself crossing Park Lane dangerously and striding towards Grosvenor Square, his Italian instincts—any man's instincts—drawing him towards his own people. The Trattoria.

Sweat pouring steadily now. Oven-hot pavements, traffic fumes, noise, bustle, grot, among the prestige offices, the galleries, the odd restaurant. Claridge's, Rolls-Royced, beflagged, beflunkeyed, kowtowing to third-world potentates with its palm out and its tongue in its cheek. The crummy end of Bond Street—Babel. Hanover Square, Regent Street, cut through Foubert's Place. Carnaby—a bad joke now; he could remember when Carnaby Street was the wonder of the world—and into Beak Street.

The Trattoria Vaccarino was still full of expense-account lunchers, the aroma at its richest and most intense—wine, herbs, garlic, olive oil, coffee. A brace of Havanas—permitted on sufferance after two-thirty. The true, luxurious, nostalgic smell of home.

Old Nonno was there, Teresa's father. Giuseppe Vaccarino, a wispy man in a cheap grey suit with an untidy moustache and hair that would be white in a year or two, was speaking atrocious, gesticulating English to one of the tables.

"*Ciao, Babbo*" (Dad). "*Telefono?*"

Old Vaccarino nodded and jerked a thumb. Frank went into the office, shook hands perfunctorily with Hector Dando, who was knee-deep in bills and cheques and cash, and rang Directory-Enquiries-Which-Town-Please?

"Upton on Severn, the police."

Put through to the desk there, he asked about Gilbert Sweet. Old friend of a friend . . . coming that way . . . friend gave me this address . . . probably out of date . . . ringing on off chance . . . wondered if you could tell . . . still there?

He was! Glory to the blessed saints, he was! Tomorrow to the land of sauce and china.

But it couldn't be tomorrow because of what happened next.

What happened was that his feet took him without conscious direction towards his father's place. (Poor old git—this business had got right on top of him. He was a sick man.) It was less than five minutes away. He must keep clear of Butter Court, but could risk it to the corner, where he could see the house, though what he hoped to gain was obscure. And CIB2? He reckoned he could spot them before they spotted him. Besides, it wasn't Antonio Corti but William non-existent Short who was supposed to have been corrupting him, and though they wouldn't have told him all that was in their tiny minds . . . He'd take a chance on it.

He was too preoccupied even to apologize when he bumped into someone coming around the corner of Butter Court. What mattered was that it wasn't CIB2. Not a rubber heel in sight. He could see the house as he approached, as shabby as its neighbours: the grime-covered brick, the sign, handsome under its patina of dirt—ANTONIO CORTI—PAINTINGS CLEANED AND RESTAURED—GALLERY (more than thirty years and he'd never corrected the spelling). The uncleaned windows, the signal jug—

The jug! Shoved hurriedly and askew to the left!

SOS!

Stuff CIB2 and all its works. He rang. No answer. He hammered. Silence. Locked. Seven-lever double-throw mortise deadlock, new and rather special. Special tools needed. Or a key. He hesitated. Then company turned up; at the double, with skipping, uneven steps and an urgent whisper. "Hurry up, boy."

"Sargey! We've got trouble."

"Locked, is it? Move over. 'Ere—spare key."

Into the passage, not big enough for a hall. Up the bare wood stairs with the creaking lurch on the sixth. Mildew, dust in nostrils, handrail loose, wallpaper ditto, with corners hanging. Landing empty. No one in the studio. "*Papà?*" No reply. "*Papà? Dove sei?*" (Where are you?) "Are you all right?"

Office—it was the office window where the jug was. Hammer on door. "*Papà?*"

Nothing.

He was in there all the same, sprawled on his back with his feet interfering with the door. Blood was draining from him, crawling over the brown lino, seeping into its cracks, its smell hanging, with the smell of fired gun, among the fusty resident odours. He was dead and Frank Short died there with him. But Franco Corti lived and suffered, to kneel and weep and swear vengeance over his father's corpse.

CHAPTER 15

MESSER SANDRO

It was perhaps a minute, perhaps an hour, before he became a detective again and asked, "Sargey, did you touch anything?"

"'Course not. Poor old codger! Poor old sod! Had it coming, didn't he? But what can you do? I mean we agreed it all. A man here nights, look in half a dozen times a day. There's *bahnd* to be a gap. Something I couldn't help, see? Couldn't help it at all . . . 'Ere, you'll have your money back. . . ."

"Rubbish. You did what you could; it's not your fault."

"I said you'd have it back, and have it back you will. Couldn't bear to touch it, could I? Besides . . ."

"Another time, Sargey, another time. Look at that."

"That" was a piece of bloodied turf lying on the dead man's chest, spilling earth on the cardigan. A small outdoor-type spider was investigating his open mouth. Flies were settling on his eyeballs. Corti closed the lids. It was hard not to shudder, touching the clammy skin.

Sargey sniffed expressively. "Grass, eh?"

"Not a bloody word. At least not to me, but that woman . . . Well, that's it. Dial 999."

"What, you? Chief bleeding Inspector? You're joking."

"I wish I was. Look, I wasn't going to tell you this, but since this morning I'm bloody suspended. Some bastard fitting me up.

Forges my signature, opens a building-society account, pays money in and pretends he's Mr. Short and I'm his son. And then he tips the wink to the rubber-heel mob and . . . I'm out, finished, had it. . . ."

"Now that's what I call defeatist. Come on, boy, you've lost a round, taken a bit of a count. So what? 'Ere—you are telling me the truth, are you? Yes, you are, all right . . ." That glare, those hunched, huge shoulders would have silenced better men than Sargey. None of your quiet bulls now; any fool could see this one was dangerous.

"Two counts, Sargey. There's this. I'm a long way down on points."

"Won't pick 'em up by moaning, will you?"

"Too right, I won't. Okay, Sargey. Seconds out."

"That's me boy. And look 'ere, you want a good corner. I'm your man, see. On the house. KayoKare at your service, sah!"

He held out a hand. "I won't argue the toss now—about the money, I mean. Meanwhile like I said. Dial 999."

He was tempted to cop out, leave Sargey to handle it, pretend he hadn't been there. But what good would that do? He could have been seen, or the Scene of Crime Boys could pick up some indication. And then there would be trouble, for Sargey as well as him. Besides, his name was bound to crop up: son, heir, copper, suspended from duty a few hours earlier. For all he knew, he might be a suspect, though with Sargey as witness . . . It was as well he hadn't been alone.

Where had they hit him? There was red on that grass, on the crumbs of soil, like the first symbolic earth on a coffin. *Bang!* through the heart, like as not. Must have been quick. *Canaglie! Figli di puttane!* Who? . . .

Who? He'd bloody bumped into him! Coming out of Butter Court not looking where he was going. Because it must have been that recent. That gun smell. Not more than a minute or two.

Now then, Franco, *think!* What did he look like? Come on, boy, trained observer like you, can't you remember *anything?* Nothing at all? . . .

The doorbell shattered his thoughts. "Mr. Levine? Police."

The explanations were as awkward as he'd expected. No one knew how to treat him—as a senior copper, a suspected villain, or simply as a murder victim's son—but once the picture was clear, they didn't seem to suspect him of the murder.

The local CID had moved in first, then the Murder Squad, and after a day or two of questions, interviews, explanations, Franco Corti had been asked politely but firmly to go away and stay there. On call; would he mind letting them know if he was away overnight? He would, but he didn't say so.

Franco Corti? Well, strictly, Frank Short, but he couldn't think of himself that way now. A Corti avenged by a Short, a mere Englishman? Ludicrous! One of the first things he did was set about recovering his name.

Time to get back in the ring. Corti versus Silverman, round four? Five? Six? What did it matter? This fight wouldn't go the distance. No decision on points but back to the old way: to a finish without gloves.

A good corner, Sargey had said, and he'd got one. Sargey himself, of course, Hector, Keith and Jackie Billings. And if Keith was to be believed, Detective Chief Superintendent Busby Papworth, your actual knight in shining, with the white rose of York stuck in his hat or, more factually, on his county cricket-club tie.

It wasn't speculation about Keith Billings. Keith had waylaid him coming out of the interview with Commander Thomas.

"Sorry, Keith, I'm out. Suspended from duty. Stitched up for bloody corruption! You'll have to look after yourself. Is that the GS list? Thanks!"

Keith had sworn under his breath, postulating the intimate habits of his superiors with rare scurrility. ". . . and he can stuff that up his dirty little botty and sit on it! So anything I can do, guv . . . Got my home phone number?"

They had exchanged numbers and addresses, and after the weekend, when Corti went out into Balfour Road to get his car and drive to Worcestershire, there was a note in it.

Just to let you know—Ayatollah Yorki's with you 100 per cent and working well. Will keep you posted. Supermum sends love.

Regards, K.

Supermum foxed him for a moment, till he remembered her nickname of "Mother Superior" when she was still Jackie Nunn. He turned the sheet over.

> *Big Titworth's the name of our Guv,*
> *Chubby cherub as sings high above.*
> *Not many can holler*
> *Like our Ayatollah*
> *Sweet blessings from Yorkssia with love.*

You had to laugh. It helped. Knowing you had friends helped too. He stuffed the note in his pocket and headed for the A40.

A40, M40. Out of London, bombing with a thousand others through the Chiltern woods, aware vaguely of the landscape, of July hot and heavy on the boughs, consolidating spring growth, getting organized for autumn . . .

Teresa!

He hadn't told her. He hadn't told a soul, only policemen and Sargey Levine, about the suspension. The murder had had its twenty-four-hour news value. It had made the front pages, TV and radio, but next day there was nothing. Of the many things that were driving him bananas, the worst was not knowing. If only he'd not been bloody suspended! They could have left it to the Squad, who were organized and equipped to tackle murder, if necessary. They mightn't have let him handle it himself because of the personal involvement, but at least he'd have known the score.

But now—nothing! He blazed his lights at some poor innocent blocking the fast lane and cut through on the inside. Not the sort of driving they teach policemen, but he wasn't one.

Past Oxford, through dreamy Cotswold villages, Tewkesbury; Upton on Severn, where you crossed the river without seeing it. Queensend, a mere hamlet. Hare Hill? "You carry straight on, look, 'bout 'arf a moile, then there's a sort of an opening, look, to the roight. It's only a farm track, moind; dunno if you'll get that car up; you want to watch out for your sump."

"Okay. Thanks."

An alien but sweet-smelling world. He left the window open.

Two hundred yards and he wound it up quickly, against a stench of unbelievable malignity. There was mud all over the road, only it wasn't mud. Cor! Was that really the lane? Muck all over it. Steep, rutted, potholed, bordered by nettles, seething with outsize flies . . .

He had to leave the car and walk, sweating buckets, and in his town shoes; his feet, geared to park and pavement, stumbling in the ruts, not always missing the gobs of yuk. At the top, the track lost its hedges and levelled out, fenced with sagging wire. To the left a ruined hovel, to the right a graceless Victorian cottage. Cowslip Close. A slum. A few weed-choked vegetables. Brambles, shacks, scrap-iron. By a thicket of nettles stood a Range Rover, no less. You'd have expected a rusting heap. The next line, he thought, begins, A *slatternly woman appeared.* . . .

She was thin, dressed in jeans and a grubby T-shirt over used, low-slung breasts; her hair drab and straggling, her face horse-like with great dark-rimmed eyes, wide full lips, no longer desirable, and not much chin. You wanted to give her five hundred quid and a good holiday. He wiped his shoes vainly on the grass.

"Excuse me; is this Mr. Sweet's house?"

A shrug. "It's where he lives." The voice was musical, educated, dead.

He hesitated. She gave him no help but stood with her eyes on him as if the effort of moving them were too much. He asked, "Should I go in then?"

"Why not?"

She had left the door ajar. He knocked. No reply. He went in, squeezing past wellies, garden tools, a twelve-bore that looked as if it hadn't been used for twenty years. The woman never moved. He could imagine her eyes fixed on the empty space where he had stood.

As soon as you saw the man, you understood her wretchedness. He sidled. He slid out of a doorway without a sound. In the dark passage his silhouette belonged to a warped Egyptian statue.

"Mr. Gilbert Sweet?"

A slightly delayed nod. Corti had his story ready. You could hardly announce yourself as a detective suspended from duty come looking for fakers. He held out a hand. "Marovitz, John Marovitz, Black Lion Gallery, Marylebone. Well, actually, we shan't be opening till after the holiday period. At present we're looking for artists, and your name cropped up, so . . ."

Gilbert Sweet spoke shyly, with an effort. "Got a card?"

Corti had. The Black Lion Gallery, just off Marylebone High Street, had lasted six months. The real Marovitz was thought to be abroad for reasons of health.

Sweet jerked his head for Corti to follow him and went back the way he had come. The room was light and high; someone had taken out the floor above, leaving the empty joist-housings in a band of unpainted brick. The upper part hadn't been touched since, but below the old ceiling the walls were blood-red, daubed one coat only over the wallpaper, with its pattern grinning through. The floor was hidden by rugs, overlapping and of every style and state of repair. A womblike, introverted den where an ego could curl up with its nose under its tail, secure in its own smell.

A den with quadraphonic hi-fi, a Scandinavian-folksy wood-burning stove, and a vast leather armchair, but also a studio. A big easel, stitched to the wall by dusty cobwebs. A kind of reading desk, with a food trolley covered with painting gear beside it. On the desk, sloping at forty-five degrees, a gesso panel, and on the panel a drawing, with the tempera underpainting half done. His nose confirmed that it was tempera, which uses yolk of egg; in the old days they used to call it *alla putrida*. For Corti, that smell, which would have sickened some men, was pure nostalgia.

There were eight or ten paintings on the walls, and each could have been an old master. Unframed, sometimes unfinished or flawed, but all with the true authority. One or two were copies, the others new to him but identifiable. Van Eyck, Duccio, Giovanni Bellini. And Brueghel—a fragment of winter countryside, a man dragging a sledge of firewood, a prancing dog . . .

He turned to Gilbert Sweet. "Impressive. Really impressive. Yours, are they?"

A sideways jerk of the head that seemed to mean yes and no at once, and a little, furtive smile. He was a proper weirdo. His head was bald on top, with a domed shining forehead, and round it his hair, grey with still a little black, spread in a crimpy wigwam over his shoulders. He was clean-shaven. That forehead looming over those wry, pinched, stunted little features made his profile almost concave. And the eyes, sheltered deep under the brows, were dark, large, and fanatical.

Fred was right. He did draw like an angel. The little half-finished painting showed it best. An *Adoration of the Magi*. It had a grace, a sureness, an eloquence of line—ravishing! The forms so solid, so *right*. And the colour—even the simple chord of the underpainting was a joy.

"Fra Angelico?" he asked.

Again the shy, self-deprecating smile, but a firm nod.

"And this?" He brought out his drawing. "I bought it in Hampstead. It is yours, isn't it?"

Sweet's face said he wasn't so sure.

"Piero di Cosimo, anyway?" This time a beam of assent.

"Marvellous! Bloody marvellous, if you'll excuse my French. And what about your own work? I mean . . ." He stopped; he could feel the man clamming up. "Yes, well, it doesn't matter. But these . . ." His arms took in the blotched crimson walls wearing his pictures like jewels. "Magnificent!"

Sweet shifted from one foot to the other, working himself up to the point of speech. "Well, of course, they're by very great masters; I mean look at them. What do you expect from Verrocchio? From Van Eyck, Bellini, Mantegna? What do you expect then? Rubbish?"

"But . . . but I thought . . ."

"You thought *I* did them? That's what everyone thinks. But let me tell you, it's not just holding a brush and dabbing on paint, you know; that's not painting, oh no. I mean any fool could do that—it's the one who's inside him, isn't it? . . ." The words, now the tap was on, shot out in a gabble, with a yowling sort of accent that was hard to follow. Holding was 'owlding, I was aw, Verrocchio Verrocchiow. A trace of Brummie? Possibly, but where . . . ?

"The one who's inside?" he asked. "What? You mean . . . ?"

"Yass. It's *them*, isn't it? It's not *me's* working on this, you know; it's the blessed Angelicow. You have to forget all about yourself, see, owpen your sowl, wait for *him* to come in. *He'll* tell you—when he's ready, I mean. And then he starts to work, and . . . You see, he's in heaven with Jesus, so you're there too. . . ." Black Country, that was it; Wolverhampton, West Brom, somewhere like that.

"Fascinating. And can you choose at all? I mean if you're working on this and suddenly it isn't Fra Angelico but Bellini?"

"Ow yass. I invite them, see. They come. When I invite them proper; not when I'm upset or anything. . . ."

"And can you pick and choose?"

"Ow yass. Mind, there's some's proper stand-offish. That Rembrandt, for a start; he doesn't want to know. Pity; he's quite good really. Well, I think he is. Clumsy, of course; he's often clumsy and he does go in for all this chiaroscuro. 'Course in his book that's the latest thing—all your drama and that; all them Dutchmen got up like Orientals in their fancy dressing-gowns." A giggle. "He gets ever so stagy, does Rembrandt. Good at his portraits, though; very good at his portraits, though I think he over-dramatizes. I tell him so, you know, and he goes off in a huff. Starts talking Dutch, you see, and what's the good of that? Does it to be rude, of course; I know he does. . . ."

Almost a Rembrandt subject. The studio lit by sunshafts from upstairs, the tall easel suggestive of a guillotine, the long-haired madman on his puppet-strings. The wife too, if she was one. Poor cow.

This was hardly the conversation of a dealer with an artist, nor was it likely to be. An idea struck him. "Would one of them do a drawing of me, do you think? This dressing wouldn't matter, would it? I get these boils, you see. . . ." The eyes softened.

"Might do. No, we needn't draw the dressing. You didn't ought to get boils; that's bad diet, that is, bad diet. Anyone special you was thinking of?"

"Botticelli? Would he come?"

The words were drying up. Only a nod this time, with the shy, gentle smile, then one last effort. "Messer Sandro isn't really happy with twentieth-century materials, but if we're nice to him . . . Would you like to sit in the armchair?"

"How long?" Corti asked. "I mean I've got to get . . ."

"Oh, very quick. I'm very deft, signor. Ask any of the fine gentlemen. . . ."

After that Corti addressed him as Messer Sandro.

It was done in twenty minutes, a perfect little Botticelli. There he was in fine red chalk, Franco Corti, man of the Renaissance, a warrior, a *condottiere*, a prince.

"Would the Maestro care to sign it?"

No, the Maestro wouldn't. Not on this nasty machine-made paper he wouldn't.

"But they do sometimes, don't they?" The face was Gilbert Sweet's again by now; it answered with smiles and twitches and shakes of the head, eked out by words: well yes, they do, but only if everything's really right.

"What about some like me? Could I sign something? Using your hands, I mean?"

Eyebrows up. A smile.

"Come on, show me. Here, give us a bit of paper. . . ." He signed *John Marovitz* with a flourish and handed pen and paper to Sweet. At the fifth try it was perfect. *John Marovitz*, scrawled as freely as he had done it himself; not a facsimile—no true signature is—but the same without a shadow of a doubt.

"Marvellous! Bloody marvellous! You know, Mr. Sweet, we really must do business together. I'd be proud to offer you a show."

A shake, almost imperceptible, of the bald, maned head, but a smiling one. Gilbert Sweet was flattered. Words began struggling to the surface. "Sorry. But you see, my own dealer . . . well, it's *business*, see? Sort of exclusive . . ."

"Your own dealer? But . . . Then why don't I know your work? May I ask who handles it?"

"It's *not* my work. I keep telling you. They don't like it, you know, if my name appears; you have to be that careful. . . ."

"Yes, I do see. Your dealer must be a very understanding man."

"Ow, he is. Ever sow understanding." But no way could he get the name. "Ow now, aw'm sorry, but it's confidential. You see, I *promised*." Not that it mattered that much, not until it was a question of proof; that signature was pretty conclusive. If he could sign *John Marovitz*, he could sign *F. Short*. From a name in a visitors' book in Duke Street.

The woman wasn't to be seen. He picked his way down the stinking lane, cleaned his shoes as best he could, and drove home. The smell was still on the car when he parked at Frank Short's gate.

CHAPTER 16

A TASTE OF HEATHER

His shoes stank too, and he'd got the stuff on his trousers. Teresa made him take them off on the doorstep and clattered off holding her nose to clean them up, martyring herself so she could blame him. If only those other stinks could be cured that easily—the Silverman stink, the Sweet stink, the murder stink. (Flies strolling between dead eyelids, dabbing, copulating, excreting—he wanted to bawl his rage to the whole world.) Teresa could deodorize his shoes, but the others were man's work. His.

"Franco!" Her voice, sharp and unpleasant, called from the side door by the dustbin.

"Yes, love?"

"The pathologist telephoned. About the post-mortem. He left a number for you to ring."

"Doctor? Short. You left a message. The post-mortem, was it?"

"Ah yes. I thought perhaps you would like to know. Unofficially, you understand."

"Yes?"

"It was a very clean death. Left ventricle. Instantaneous. No suffering . . . Are you there?"

"Sorry—just taking it in. No suffering. I'm glad. No, I'm not, I'm . . . I'm . . . I suppose if he had to die, it was a good way. Well, better than some . . ."

"Better than . . . Had you noticed any change in his voice?"

"Sort of brassy? Yes."

"Bronchial carcinoma, Mr. Short."

"Bronchial carci——? Lung cancer?" No wonder he looked like death.

"I'm afraid so. He couldn't have gone on much longer; these things develop awfully fast, you know. . . ."

"How long then?"

"Weeks. Perhaps only days. One can't be exactly specific. He'd have suffered quite a lot. So I thought perhaps if I told you, you might come to see this, shocking as it is, as a sort of kindness. . . ."

"Yes. Yes. I see." So if I get my hands on that murdering bastard, I might just do a sort of kindness myself and break his neck before his jaw instead of after.

Lung cancer? Did the old man know? Probably not; he'd have no reason to hide it. Or did he just tell Denise? What's it matter? He's dead. You can have your woman to yourself now. If you want her. Death, suspension, vendetta, the survival-fight. Storm winds. End of summer. Short hot summer of love. Fine old thunderstorm brewing out there. Symbolic. Time the weather broke anyway—garden needs rain . . . Oh hell. Oh bloody, bloody hell.

The weather did break. It pelted and blew and thundered half the night. The best you could say was that in the morning the car smelt less. Bad campaigning weather. Too bad. The Silverman front.

He marched into the gallery as bold as brass, in his tight black Franco Corti suit and blacker hat. *Hommages à Flandres* was gone; instead there was a mixed show—Silverman's few living artists with a sprinkling of English Post-Impressionist. Vee's work more than holding its own; a marble child-portrait by her father ditto. Fiona emerged from the office—slim, dark, fragrant, with her starry blue eyes. Ought to be out striding the heather, dogs at heel. "Hello," he said.

"Franco!" She was genuinely pleased. "What have you done to your neck?"

"Boils. Not very glamorous. How's things?"

She screwed up her face at the office door and put her tongue out.

"I'm sorry." He wasn't; the more anti-Silverman she was, the better. "Look, I was passing on my way to lunch. I got this crazy idea—come and join me."

It worked. Couldn't stay long, but a pizza or something would be great. Any time—now, if he liked; it was a quarter to one. She rang through to let Silverman know. ". . . Back by half past? Thanks."

Three quarters of an hour. "Shepherd Market?" he said. "Little Italian place; nothing posh but the cannelloni are quite something. Okay?"

The weather was grey and showery, but she took it for granted they would walk. He liked that. He liked having her beside him. She was somehow clean—not ponced up in some poodle-parlour but . . . well, clean. Wholesome, country-fresh. Those were the words they used for selling factory food; they ought to get her on their programmes. . . .

"Silverman trouble?" he asked.

"Not really. I just . . . Oh, I don't know. I just don't like him."

He made sympathetic noises. ". . . You said once you wondered if he was all above-board. Nothing new in that direction, is there?"

"Don't think so. Why?"

"Well . . . Listen, this is between you and me. No one else, right?"

"Mm." She nodded. As good as a sworn statement, he reckoned, and better than most.

"Well, we do have one or two doubts. I mustn't say more than that, but we do. Nothing concrete, but . . . Anyway, I'll tell you one thing: If your boss is up to no good, it won't be just fiddling his expenses."

"Well, honestly, I'm not surprised. And you're right, he wouldn't just dabble. Oh gosh! I wonder if he *is* doing—whatever it is."

"That's what we want to find out." They were in Piccadilly now; the pavement by the Green Park bus stop was crowded, and they fell into single file. It wasn't till they were at their plastic-topped table, with the cannelloni on order and a half-litre of the dry Lambrusco which was special here because the *padrone* was from Romagna, that he came back to the subject.

"Okay? I'm afraid the seats are a bit cramped, but . . ."

"Oh, but it's lovely. It isn't all phoney like some of them." The Trattoria Vaccarino had plastic vines all over the ceiling, plastic lobsters by the cash desk, and king-size Chianti flasks on the tables.

"Silverman," he said when the cannelloni and, more important, the Lambrusco were finished and he judged she was feeling receptive.

"What about him? Look—why did you tell me all that? How do you know I won't go and warn him like a loyal employee?"

"Because you said you wouldn't. I'll tell you why I let on. I hoped perhaps you might be able to help—that is, if you'd like to. I mean I couldn't possibly expect you to if you didn't feel . . ."

"Tell me more."

"All right. Look, we haven't any evidence. We can't go swearing out search-warrants and marching in at the front door. But seriously, we do want to know . . ."

She was really listening now, coffee cup in mid-air.

"Now I don't know if you know this, but we can't always do these things by the book, and in a situation like this . . . Look, what I really want is to get in and have a look round. That's all. At night, perhaps, or a weekend. It's not allowed, of course; I'd do it at my own risk—I mean if I'm captured, my neck's on the block; doesn't matter who winked at it in the first place, he'd have to play the axeman for his own sake, for the sake of the Force. . . ." (Understatement of the year; it'd be prison.)

"But . . . but you'd never get inside. I mean the security locks, the alarms . . . The place is like a bank vault."

"I've no doubt it is, and that's why I'm asking for your help. If you can get the details for me . . . I mean we're policemen, we do know a bit about these things; and once you know what you're up against . . ."

What he was up against, she told him, was armour-plate glass, some sophisticated locks, an alarm actuated by outside doors and windows and by pressure-pads under the carpets. No problem, not if she was around to let you in; no problem at all.

The difficulty was the private stock-room behind Silverman's office. No key. "And I'm not even sure that's how it works. I don't think there's even a keyhole. Oh, there *must* be. D'you know, I honestly can't remember. I'll look this afternoon and let you know. . . . Oh gosh—look at the time! I must run. Look— I'll ring you tonight. Thanks for a super lunch. See you, Franco."

She didn't phone; she turned up. Teresa, thank heaven, was at Beak Street. He shivered at what it would have been like otherwise.

She had put on a skirt so short it was almost a mini. He hadn't really noticed her legs before, but they were good ones. Long and slim but not skinny. Skirts like that were asking for trouble. Trouble? Nice figure too. What you might call understated, but okay. And that perfume—she'd put on an awful lot of it. Yes. Great. "Gin?" he asked. "Gin and tonic?"

"Super."

Instinct, then her breath, told him she'd had at least one already. He was right; after the next she was telling him the story of her life; one more and she was crying wetly on his shoulder.

Silverman-trouble, parent-trouble, boy-trouble; it was common-place enough. It'd pass. All she needed was a shoulder. At least that was what he thought till she lay back on the settee and the skirt rode up her thighs and instead of pulling it down again she pulled it up.

That moment was a turning point in a way, because in spite of the Eyetie backlash he didn't move in. He could hardly believe it when he heard himself say, "Now, now. That's no way for a lady to behave. Come on, love; sit up and make yourself presentable."

And she did, and it wasn't long before she was herself again and giving him a sisterly kiss and saying thank you. "I won't for-get that, Franco. I was behaving like a tart and you put me in my place so nicely. I'd have felt awful, you know, if . . ."

"Don't give it another thought, darling. You'll be all right. Now what about that private stock-room. Any joy?"

"There *is* a keyhole."

"Any idea where the key's kept?"

"'Fraid not. In his pocket, I should think."

"In his desk, perhaps? That's it. It was in his desk. I re-member."

"Was? Oh, d'you mean the first time you . . . When you asked about the Boucher?"

"Right. Wanted to see what he'd got in that stock-room, didn't I, and he was on his way to open up when . . . But I remember now; he'd a key in his hand, and he'd taken it out of his desk. Right-hand side, I think."

"Super." She smiled, less nervously this time.

"And talking of that Boucher, someone said it was sold to a man called—what was it?"

"Morrison? I think it was Morrison."

Alias Blamey; Scouse-Irish and out for blood. Grr! He had to control his voice. "There wouldn't be an invoice?"

"I expect so. Do you want details?"

"It'd be useful. Do you know if there's been any contact since? We were rather hoping for a word with friend Morrison—not that that's his real name. But he doesn't seem to be around."

"D'you know, I think he was in. About a week ago; in Mr. Silverman's office."

"Oh, he was, was he? You don't know what they talked about? Of course not; how could you?"

"Sorry." She shook her head. "Oh yes, I do remember one thing. That man that was killed, the restorer, Mr. Corti, he used to do work for Mr. Silverman. . . ." (All life in him went quiet, fused into one still, acute sensor, one concentrated, silent waiting.) "Mr. Silverman rang for some coffee, but I didn't answer straight away, a customer wouldn't stop talking. I was holding the phone in mid-air, and d'you know, just as I was putting it to my ear I thought I heard that name—sort of in the background."

"What name? Corti?"

"Did you know him?"

"A bit. Yes; you could say I knew him. What were they saying?"

"Sorry. I didn't . . ."

He clenched his teeth for a moment, then changed the subject. "The alarms, darling. They can't be on all day, obviously. So . . ."

"There's a switch. Whoever leaves last switches them on."

"What about the door you go out by?"

"The front door? That one doesn't come on till you turn the key; there's an electric contact or something."

He nodded. "What we call a shunt lock. And the master switch; where's that?"

"Just inside." She explained how in the morning you had to open the door and keep off the mat till you'd unlocked the little wall-safe and turned off the main switch inside.

"That's really useful. Listen, darling. One of these fine evenings you wouldn't lend me your keys? I'd drop them off either late at night or early morning. Silverman won't know a thing."

She wasn't too sure, but then people like her were brought up to be loyal.

"Look, if Silverman's bent, then surely . . . Like a soldier doesn't have to obey orders if they're illegal." (He'd got that from Sargey Levine.) "Mustn't obey them, actually, or you could get Belsen or something. And if Silverman's not bent, then what's the harm? After all, this isn't just the art market, is it? What you told me about Morrison, and I've seen that guy's track record . . . Let's face it, darling: They could have been talking about murder."

"Oh *no!* D'you know, the day that murder was in the papers, Mr. Silverman was really shaken; wandering around like a lost soul, moaning about poor old Antonio. I've never seen him like that. It was odd, really. They were only what you might call business associates, but he was carrying on as if it was someone really close."

"Putting on an act?"

"His acts aren't like that; he just goes extra pompous. No, this wasn't put on. He was shattered."

"What'd do that to our Max? A guilty conscience?"

"Not exactly. He was so—you know—so *surprised.* And cross with himself, I thought. As if he'd knocked someone over in the car . . ."

An accident? That didn't make sense. People did get shot accidentally—an empty gun and that—but not people like Antonio Corti, and not in places like Butter Court, and not with bits of turf plonked on the wound. So why should Silverman . . . ?

She was young; maybe she had misread Silverman's mood. It would take more than Fiona Rattray to convince Franco Corti he wasn't behind it. Silverman and Blamey—the friendly Russian and the daft bloody Mick.

It had been a sad little evening. When she got up to go she avoided his eye. Her face was sort of dishevelled, though it was an hour since she stopped crying. She kissed him goodbye chastely, then on the doorstep turned and clutched him tight and kissed him again, brashly, crudely, hard. It was over before he had time to respond, and she was saying, " 'Bye, Franco," in a voice gone small and shaky. "And thanks for—oh, everything."

He watched her walk away on her long legs and pictured moors and heather and bounding dogs. Poor kid, he thought; poor kid. And as for you, Franco Corti, turning down a chance like that . . . When you think of Denise . . . This one'd have been so fresh. A glass of water frae the burn compared with absinthe. Wouldn't poison you like absinthe. Why not, Franco Corti? Call yourself a man?

It dawned on him that he could.

Hector Dando grinned over the private dining table. "Okay. I get it."

"When, then?"

"When you wish it. Tonight? Tomorrow?"

Corti rang Fiona at the gallery, who cooed like an upper-class dove. He made suitable noises back, then asked, "Those keys, darling; you remember you said . . ."

She spoke rapidly and low. "When do you want them?"

"Sooner the better. Tonight? When d'you close? Half past five? Anyone stay late?"

"Not very often. Why?"

"Could you let us in, soon as the others are gone, then leave us to get on with it?"

"All right."

"Great. Ring me when you're ready." He gave the Trattoria's number. "It's quite close. See you, darling. Thanks."

He turned to Dando. "Tonight. Okay?"

"Okay." Hector's eyes, sheltering behind their big specs, didn't exactly grin with the rest of his face, but they registered. Meanwhile they kept scanning. Those eyes took in a lot.

He left the Trattoria after lunch and exhibition-crawled till it was time to fetch the Maxi and find a meter near the Trattoria where it could stay all night if it had to. It was after half-past five when he let himself in, taking it for granted he was tailed. It was what he would have done in their nasty rubber-heeled shoes. The countermeasures had occurred to him and Hector simultaneously.

Hector was waiting. They ducked into the private dining alcove, and Hector produced the gear. Driving gloves, the finest, thinnest leather, okay for handling paper. A camera disguised as a packet of fags, loaded with 8-mm cine film. "So fast is supersonic," Hector said. Very handy.

Ten minutes later Fiona rang. Corti said to stand by to let them in in five minutes. Quick. No hanging about on pavements. Seconds later they were edging past the kitchen waste bins and out.

CHAPTER 17

ACT OF WAR

The car was waiting in the mews at the back, an inconspicuous middle-aged Chevette with an inconspicuous middle-aged driver, organized by Hector. CIB2 would have to be uncommonly interested to deploy resources for covering the Trattoria, front and back, as well as him.

The traffic had eased. In no time the driver whipped round the corner from Ryder Street and slammed on his brakes, and they were inside the Silverman. A tailing car would have had to be impossibly close to see them.

Inside, with his hands sweating into his gloves, he introduced his allies. Hector kept quiet. An Italian accent was not in order for Sergeant Jones of the Metropolitan Police.

Corti put an arm round Fiona's shoulders. "Right, darling. Show us what you can."

She started with the alarms. No problem. No need to point out the pressure-mats, or anything but the master switch in its unlocked wall-safe. Next, the boss's office, also unlocked. His leather-topped desk was less than tycoon-sized. Queen Anne, you'd have said, and genuine, if you hadn't known desks like that weren't made in that century.

The keys of the private stock-room should be in the right-hand pedestal. He tried a drawer. Locked. All drawers locked. Hector was ready with skeleton keys, and either lucky or exceptionally good, because it was open at the third try.

Fiona said, "Amazing!"

Corti said, "Nice work, Sergeant," and Hector smiled and looked smug.

"Don't you ever talk?" she asked him.

Corti cut in before he could answer. "Not much. Right, darling, we'll take that one from here when you've gone. Now then, the office. There won't be anything out of line, but there's one or two ledger cards . . ."

She knew where to look. Sales ledger: M for Morrison, click. Bought ledger: S for Sweet, no card; C for Corti, click; D for delle, B for Bandenere; no cards. All microfilmed and in Hector's pocket before Corti had more than glanced at them. Which was precisely why he'd brought him so that he needn't waste time reading. He'd suspected Hector would be organized for jobs like this, and when he'd asked him point-blank at lunch time and then invited him along, Hector's eyes had been as near lighting up as he'd seen them.

They could lose Fiona now. He kissed her politely and took the bunch of keys, plus her address for dropping them off. "It'll probably be the sergeant. He won't disturb you, just pop them through the letter-box, right?"

That was okay by her, sharing a mews house with friends. The keys would be safe on the mat.

It was a bright evening, with three hours' daylight left. He felt easier now they had finished in the front, where they could be seen from the street. He homed, tense with anticipation, on Silverman's desk.

They found the key to the private stock-room in the top drawer of the right-hand pedestal. The rest could wait; what mattered was behind that heavy mahogany door. Its lock moved sweetly under the key. He turned the cut-glass knob and opened it—onto a blank, drab wall a foot from his nose.

Even Hector swore a little. The wall had no skirting and was tight up to the door frame. Dead to the ear, cold to the touch, like a safe.

"Steel shutter?" he asked in Italian. Hector's English conversation could wait. They were Italians now, patron and client, members of a family pursuing the family interest.

"*Naturalmente*. The question is how to move it."

Brute force would be hopeless and would leave traces; there was no knob, no keyhole, no visible control. No particle-beams, no pressure-mats. No nothing.

They spoke simultaneously. "The desk?" "A hidden switch?"

In the kneehole, under the desk-top? Behind the drawers? Concealed in the carved border or the tooling of the leather? In the reading-lamp, the drawer-fronts, the phones? They went over that desk millimetre by millimetre. Not a thing. Finally they lifted each pedestal in turn and looked underneath. No wires except the obvious flexes. Nothing.

"But it had to be the desk," Corti said. "That other time, he was walking towards that door with the key in his hand. . . . But if he hadn't already opened that panel . . ."

"Perhaps he had not. Perhaps he was going to."

Corti shrugged. "How? He'd want to keep the button secret, but there he was on his way to open up with me watching him like a cat."

"*Vediamo*." (Let's see.) "Something on the door, perhaps, or on the frame?"

They fiddled with the knob, the lock, the escutcheon; they tried the striking-plate. They climbed on a chair to inspect the top. They pushed all the mouldings of all the panels in all the directions. *Niente*.

He sat down on Silverman's chair to think. The door was still open, and Hector was playing around with the hinges, but they'd done that already. The hinges were just hinges, the screws just screws. . . .

Hector withdrew, pushed the door gently shut, and fiddled some more. "*Ecco, Ispettore. Entri!*"

Corti yanked the door open, peered into half-lit space and whispered, "How the devil did you do that?"

"Look, you must shut it. Now—what do you see that is unusual?"

With the door closed, the big brass knuckles of the hinges stood out towards you. One, two, three best-quality heavy brass butt hinges . . .

Three hinges? Why three?

What you had to do was prod the underside of the middle one with a pen or a key or something, and it was at the perfect height for doing so inconspicuously. Corti prodded, opened the door and the shutter was closed again; repeated the exercise and it was open, the hook-bolts that had held it showing recessed in the door-frame. He switched on the lights.

For an instant he was Stout Cortez on the high Sierras, Armstrong on the moon. The room had no windows and smelt of expensive cigars. A Spanish leather screen divided the storage from the near end, where the walls were flock-papered and the pictures must have come from Georgian brothels. Friend Max's little nest, cosy, kinky, expensive; too ponced-up and Regency by half, and as self-expressive as Sweet's ego-hole or Willison's boudoir.

Beyond the screen, racks of pictures covered the left-hand wall, with open shelving opposite, and between them two of those glorified portfolios on stands that galleries use for prints. The shelves were empty except for three sculptures gathering dust. Corti knew about those. Child pornography, but you couldn't get him for them, they were too good. Artistic merit. Yuk.

He glanced in a portfolio. Prints. Modernistic dirt this time, but plausibly with artistic merit. Angrily, hating his reactions, he slammed it shut and opened its twin. The prints here were old masters, plausible as well, but too many and too good—like nine identical Rembrandt etchings. Nine! And an early state too. He'd never have pulled nine like that. Evidence, but for official proceedings, not his own. He went back past the screen to the office space.

The writing table must be worth thousands; brass-mounted, brass-inlaid, with a fine mahogany grain. Green leather top, green silk lampshade, green leather chair. Telephones and a portable typewriter stood on the table, and beside it a filing cabinet, locked. He found his tension tool, opened his matchbox of jigglers, and went to work, watched indulgently by Dando.

It only took two minutes. The top drawer was empty except for stationery and a red plastic ring binder full of poetry. Poetry! Some in an ornate and prissy longhand, some typed. "To Elsa," "Circe," "Brazilian Journey"—he'd go there, wouldn't he? His letterheads proclaimed *Silverman International, London, Paris, New York, Milan, Venice, São Paolo.* Fancy old Max writing poetry. He couldn't judge it except that the style was mixed; some of it de-dum de-dum with rhymes, some just prose chopped up short like left-over spaghetti. Not evidence and not his scene. He left it on the table and opened the lower drawer.

This one did hold files—a few. They got down to microfilming, with Hector clicking away as fast as Corti could feed him the material. It seemed hours before the last folder was back in place. It had been too quick for reading more than snippets, but there had been accounts, business letters, addresses. The files were in the usual sliding concertina. He pushed it back and looked underneath.

That was where the cash was, in tidy bundles. Swiss francs, Deutschmarks, dollars, cruzeiros; all sorts. Hardly worth a photo, though a year or two back it could have put friend Max in the dock.

Next the typewriter. He loaded it with paper, a new sheet of carbon, a flimsy, and typed all the letters—capitals and lower case —all the numbers, all the punctuation marks, then some half-remembered sentences about building society deposits, and pocketed the end-product, carbon and all, before turning to the paintings.

Erotica again, ranging from girlie titillation to twisted, blood-soaked evil. But by people who knew how to paint. More artistic merit.

It was a double-decker rack, the pornography below. Above, there were fewer pictures, arrayed at right angles to the wall between their slats. He slid one out, careful of its frame. Nothing pornographic here, but a seascape with ships. Dutch, 1700, give or take; if he'd had to guess, he'd have said Willem van de Velde the Younger, and for marine work, apart from Turner, which was a different world, that meant tops.

He summoned Hector, who had his nose into Silverman's poems, to start photographing again. They went down the rack, picture by picture. Nice stuff; things that, if they were right—which he didn't believe for a moment—would fetch five to fifty grand at Sotheby's, with the odd one pushing six figures.

He put back a little *Flight into Egypt* from the predella of some Tuscan altarpiece. The next was similar in size. He edged it gently from its rack and nearly dropped it. "*Dio mio!* Hector, look at this! Do you know what this is?"

The herald angel, rainbow-winged, in a vermilion robe, the Virgin in blue, the fragments of arch and landscape, courtesy of the blessed Fra Giovanni Angelico da Fiesole.

Hector goggled through his glasses. "You will take it?"

Corti shook his head. "No. Pity, but no. It's evidence here. Besides, he could miss it and scarper."

"Is true. So you have your evidence."

He was conscious of a slight grogginess. His pulse. It was going like the clappers! Must have some fresh air soon. He gulped a heart-capsule, but without water it glued itself to his throat. "Not enough, Hector. Evidence he's got his hands on a stolen picture, but not that he knows it's stolen. No evidence he's fitted me up. And nothing about my father."

"Then perhaps you should read this." Hector leafed through the book of poetry. "*Ecco, qui!* I do not understand it all, but I think it has relevance."

It was a rough draft with many crossings-out. The title had been "Murder in the Cathedral," then "Murder in the Studio," then "The Paddy Factor," before finishing as "For AC."

> *Old friend, old workman of unerring hand,*
> *Of flawless eye, of magisterial skill*
> *Learnt, who knows how, on high Parnassus hill,*
> *Brought, who knows why, to grace this graceless land;*
>
> *Old friend, old fox, who danced your saraband*
> *Unseen, not let your hidden casket spill*
> *One jewel before swine, nor bent your will*
> *To wind nor tide, nor heeded man's command—*
>
> *Old friend, old confidant, discretion's mould*
> *Till bitch Pandora with discretion's key*
> *Unlocked the coffer, loosed the winds and sold*
> *Our secrets, till, discretion reft from me,*
> *I blurted, "Who will rid me, who will rid . . . ?"*
> *Of you, poor friend!*
>   *And black-souled villainy did.*

He put it down because he was finding it hard to hold it steady, then read it again, and the more he read it, the more it tallied. The first bit was just a roundabout way of saying Antonio Corti, but the second . . . Pandora's box held trouble. Bitch Pandora—

Denise? Did he know about Denise? Because if he did . . . He must have. There it was in black and white; she sold their secrets, and if that wasn't her who was it?

And the crossed-out title. *The Paddy Factor.* Your daft bloody Mick.

He tried to speak, but his voice wouldn't work, and it wasn't just the capsule stuck in his throat. He pulled himself together, tried again and made it. "Hector—have you microfilmed it?"

Hector nodded and looked understanding.

"Come on. Wrap it up. I've had enough of this place." Being in Silverman's own foxhole, with his secret things and thoughts was like being inside his head. Nasty.

Though seemingly Max had a conscience. Big deal. Don't you start shedding tears over Silverman, Franco Corti. If you cried for every villain who's part human or damages someone by mistake, you'd never stop. He set you up, didn't he? He had your father killed, or he thought he had, though that Scouse had more cause of his own. And to crown it he's got your Fra Angelico.

Life stretch for you, Maxie boy.

Evidence, he thought, tossing in bed that night and trying not to wake Teresa. Evidence of what? Evidence he's got a bent picture. And some phoney etchings. Evidence he had anything to do with Papà's death? Not law-court evidence, except maybe a bit of corroboration. Enough to get him investigated? Yes. Enough to go in and pull him? Good question, but probably yes, on account of the etchings. But no evidence of fitting up Frank Short or whoever I was. Depends what's on that film, doesn't it?

Old friend, old comrade, fox, confidant. Were they really that close? Or a bit of artistic licence? What's it matter? He's dead and Max triggered it. That's what matters. And if I get my hands on that smooth, smug . . . I might, too, since that raid.

Raid? A big word, but why not? Raids could be acts of war as well as of policemen. They'd gone rapidly through Silverman's outer office before leaving but found nothing, and if they had spent half the night with Hector's camera, they'd probably still have found nothing. So Hector had phoned up his transport, and they had closed down the private stock-room (with Corti doing his nut about leaving his picture and that poetry), closed down the Queen Anne–type desk, set the alarms, and walked out, carefully locking the front door, and into the waiting car.

It was still daylight, the sun catching chimneys and roofs and striking warm and low across Piccadilly. At half past eight Corti was helping Sylvie with her homework before going down to eat, and Hector had taken the car to Chiswick with Fiona's keys. At half past ten, Corti, full of *bistecca alla Florentina* and Chianti, left the Trattoria with his wife on his arm, collected the maxi—plus tail, if any—and drove home.

He couldn't sleep. Denise. What about Denise? Twenty-three thousand quid, that's what. Payoff. Frank Short's payoff next. Resignation? Redundancy? Neasden? Papà's money; his pictures. Is there a will? Ought to be a will. What's CI playing at? (CI equals Murder Squad.) Had the case a week—not a word. Must be *something* to go on. That man—Butter Court—bumped into him . . . "*Gesù Maria!*" He had said it aloud. Teresa turned over and cursed him sleepily. "*Gesù Maria!*" he repeated under his breath. His stupid, over-active brain had thrown up an image, a trained eye's snapshot: a long, slung, pointed jaw; a sharp, bony nose with the mouth close beneath it; eyes blue, close, and deep under frowning gingery brows; hair sandy, professionally waved and set, hiding the ears; height five ten, weight twelve stone; age thirty-five, forty. Open-neck shirt, ventilated shoes, well-pressed slacks, and this gabardine jacket, all swank and shoulders like a banana-republic uniform. Enough there to be really useful. Must tell them, tomorrow, first thing.

He slid ultra-carefully out of bed and crept downstairs to write it down.

CHAPTER 18

WHAT GOES INTO COFFINS

Looking back afterwards at the weeks that followed, you had to use logic to sort out what had happened when. Those unending microfilm sessions. The vitriol-thrower's trial. Carrozza. Silverman. The arrest. The end of the children's term and his father's will and that monstrous accountant, and Butter Court, and putting the property up for sale. The Gervase Willison story; the rain-soaked nightmare. And at some time in the middle, the official change back to Franco Corti.

The microfilm yielded, first, correspondence with Gilbert Sweet about unspecified and unrecorded deliveries. Second, the ledger card of J. Morrison, Esq., of Dulwich, on which the only entry was the sale of *Portrait of a Lady* by François Boucher for £65,000—half the asking price and maybe a third of what it would have been if it were genuine.

Third, the ledger card of Antonio Corti, which showed the purchase of *Portrait of a Lady* by Boucher (not François, not even F., but just the surname, which could have been a whim of the typist but usually meant *non-Boucher*) for £25,000. That was £25,000 almost pure profit for his father, who would have picked the thing up for a song. ("In *terrible* condition, Franco. I don't say Boucher . . .") And £40,000 not so pure profit for Silverman with his overheads and his taxes, because he was bound to pay on what went through his ledgers. So at the end of the day perhaps fifty-fifty? Probably. You must be sharp to get that much out of friend Max; he felt a Florentine but unpolicemanlike pride in his father's acumen.

There were a few similar purchases, plus fees, fat ones, for cleaning and restoration. For the last twelve months it added up to £73,000—seven or eight times his own pay—and Silverman wasn't the old man's only source of cash. Hm.

Fourth, from the microfilm, a folder labelled "Provenances," with photocopies of ancient documents. That was a weird one, because it was incomplete, and you'd expect the provenance of a work to be filed with the other stuff about it. Also it was in the holy of holies and not even in Silverman's ordinary office. Which suggested those provenances were special. Specially commissioned?

He thumbed through the documents, which were in many languages and sometimes difficult scripts, and studied the Italian ones in more detail. He was no scholar, and the archaic wording was often beyond him when he could read it, but a certain amount came through. For example, that one paper appeared to be a letter from Sandro Botticelli to a more or less illustrious patron called Lorenzo, asking for his money for the patron's portrait. And another in English, headed Villa Bandenere, began, *Dear Ruskin*, and was signed, Wm. Cunningham.

He whipped them smartly round to the Gruenwald, where they hummed and hawed and scratched their heads and telephoned and looked up references for half a morning, and finally decided they had doubts about Cunningham, but the Botticelli letter looked okay. Then one of their students wandered in and cast an eye on it and announced, "That's odd."

"Oh?" asked the lady called Miranda.

"The wording. It's identical with one of Michelangelo's to

Pope Julius; I swear it is. I've been working on the correspondence for my thesis. Where's the original?"

"You tell us," said Corti.

Fifth and last, and this was the big one, a letter dated six weeks
ago. He got out the specimen sheet he had typed on Silverman's
machine and he could see no difference in the type. He didn't
think Forensic would either.

It was a carbon of the letter Commander Thomas had shown
him, from not-William Short to the Mayfair and Marylebone
Building Society.

A strange feeling invaded him, an awareness at once of relaxing
and of deep emotion. Deliverance . . . triumph . . . joy. Evidence foolproof and infallible, sitting in that filing cabinet ready
for the Force to go in and collect it. Evidence that with a bit of
support would convict Max Silverman as surely as if he'd been
caught red-handed. Evidence to wipe the corruption-smear. But
not its memory. That was the scar, and like the burn on his neck,
it was there for life. The copper who was suspended for graft.
Ironical, really, because one of the things that had made him so
sure about Silverman was the farthing's damages that were supposed to clear his name. Ironical indeed, for him and Silverman
to be in the same nasty boat. Except Silverman was a villain.
When Franco Corti broke the law, it was to do justice. . . .

Broke the law? Same boat as Silverman? What would Frank
Short make of that? Frank Short, with his lawnmower and fish
and chips and tea; with his sludged-up arteries and his constipated puritanical soul? Who cared about Frank Short? This
was men's business.

"Keith? Short here. How's it going?" He was in the Trattoria,
praying the phone wasn't bugged, which he judged a lesser risk
than being furtive in call-boxes.

"Good question. Well, now—A & A's going to the dogs, Titworth's going off the deep end, villains from strength to strength, and life just on. *Obladi, Oblada, life goes o-on! Dah diddle diddle dee dah . . ."*

He resisted the temptation to join his chief in the deep end. "And my old guv'nor? Anything from CI?"

"Not a chance. Sorry."

"And the other lot—rubber heels and that?"

"Same again. Close to the chest. I mean how else . . . ?"

"Only asking. Listen, Keith, could you do me a favour?"

"Sure, if I can."

"Look, you say the Guv's on my side. I've got this piece of evidence. You know what they produced against me? No? Someone set up a building-society account in my name. They typed a letter, and I've a specimen sheet off the machine we think typed it. Could you give it to the Guv for me? I'd rather do it that way than write in. No need to say where you got it unless he pushes you . . ."

"He won't; I'm pretty sure he won't."

"And tell him this, Keith. There's more to come. Not just for the rubber-heel mob; for A & A. CI too, I shouldn't wonder."

"That's great, that's really great. Will do."

"Thanks. But don't come near me, not yet. I'll drop it off for you. Down the East End, right?" He gave the address of Kayo-Kare.

"Okey-dokey, guv. Does this mean you're in the clear then?"

"Should do. But you tell me. How do I know what they've been fed?"

"Anyway, the best of British luck. That it then?"

"Not quite. When you're at Kayo, could you drop off a photo of Blamey for me? And a reminder of his description?"

"No problem. Why? Are you on to something?"

"I'll tell you when I've seen the Blamey stuff. Thanks anyway. See you."

He went to Whitechapel straight from the phone, carrying his sheet of typing in a jumbo-sized envelope, and found Sargey looking glum. "Can't help it, Frankie. I feel responsible."

"Rubbish. You did what you undertook to do. We knew the risks, all of us. And what do you think I feel? My war, Sargey. My old guv'nor."

"Vendetta, eh? And you changed your name to Short."

"That won't last much longer, I can tell you."

"It's no good, Frankie. Once a Yid, always a Yid; once an Eyetie, always an Eyetie. Might as well admit it, mightn't you? I mean, look at me. Married a goy, talk like a goy, live like a goy. Why, I even go to church. But I know flipping well what I am. My own people, Frankie."

"I know." It was reassuring to have it put into words for him. "Yes, you could call it a vendetta—only I wouldn't use a knife or anything. If I'd only thought, Sargey—a few quid more and you could have done a twenty-four-hour job. . . ."

"How long could we have kept that up? No, Frankie, it's not the money, it's that poor old man. And losing. I never cared for losing. Listen, I'm not keeping the money, you know that. . . ."

They argued for half an hour, and at the end Corti gave in. "Okay. It'll go to charity, mind."

"You know what? If you'd turned it down, I'd have done the same."

Money. His father's will. It had arrived by registered post from the Yard, together with a bundle of cash and financial papers, addressed to *Executors of A. Corti*. The executors, it told him, were he and one Bruce Zappaterra, who lived in Highgate and seemed to be his father's "dear and valued client who is also an accountant." A raddie like himself but from the Veneto, so half a foreigner and about as straight as the maze at Hampton Court. He was glad the will had come to him, because the cash was fifty grand and he didn't like to think what could have stuck to those dear, valued, manicured hands.

You couldn't imagine those hands dirty. Bruce Zappaterra dressed to kill and smelt of cigarettes and stale aftershave. He had a gaunt, grey-brown face and a nicotined moustache of the same colour. His name wasn't in the professional registers, and Corti's first experience of him was when he phoned and Zappaterra asked him to lunch at the Tiberio, where it costs you, and failed to pick up the bill.

The papers were a complicated mess. After much thought he photocopied them at the Post Office and gave Zappaterra the originals. After all, he had been the old man's tax adviser, and the hassles over VAT and income tax alone made his hair stand on end. He kept the cash to himself till they went hand in hand to open their joint account (Exors. of A. Corti) and pay it in.

The will itself was straightforward. The pictures and the Butter Court freehold came to him, the residue (six figures before tax) to his children. The tax was an unknown quantity. Tens of thousands certainly, and for all he knew hundreds. The whole thing frightened him, as if over his new fortune in pictures hung some great black Aberfan slide waiting for the storm.

Then there was Gudgeon's trial for the vitriol. With his form, he got five years for GBH, but he still hadn't talked, and no one said a word about Blamey or murder or anything. And as for Denise . . .

No, he told himself firmly. It's indecent, it's immoral, it's unwise. Scheming little bitch. And no more use as a snout. She as good as killed him herself. Does she realize that? He watched her in the box and couldn't tell. Demure, chic, composed; confident of the Court's sympathy. No questions about what she was doing in the park on a chief inspector's arm; nothing about her insurance rewards. Just a perky little hen sparrow that had lost some tail feathers to an alley cat and grown new ones already. There were moments during that trial when he wanted to roar like a bull, to charge in and send them all flying, to tell the whole pussyfooting gang of them the truth. Only he couldn't prove it yet.

One good thing was that no one mentioned his suspension, though surely they knew. There was an awkward moment when he had to give his name and rank, but the lawyers left it alone. He felt quite kindly to lawyers after that.

Was that before or after the two trips to Kayo, to drop the type-writer specimens and collect Billings's Blamey material? He opened the envelope with hands he could barely stop trembling, under a barrage of good-humoured chatter from Sargey's Florrie.

One look was enough. No question. That long, thin jaw, slightly undershot in profile, the close-set eyes, the little mouth tucked under the sharp nose. Bumped into him, hadn't he? Bumped into his father's murderer and never noticed a thing. You'd have thought some instinct, some Willisonian informed feel would have alerted him, that he'd have felt a compulsion to clobber the man, or at least pay attention. If only life worked like that. It'd be a lot easier for policemen.

He skimmed through the description. Hair, sandy; eyes, blue; ears, large, sticking out slightly (which you could see from the mug-shots, anyway). Height, weight, age, all close to his esti-mates. Dermot Ignatius Blamey, Scouse, villain, and mortal foe. Having the pictures in his hand gave him a feeling of power over the man, as if he could black-magic him with them or something if he knew how.

He thanked the Levines and left, brooding in the tube home on his campaign. The intelligence side was pretty well wrapped up, the arch-enemies pinpointed: Silverman first, and now Bla-mey. And Sweet? An enemy but fundamentally a mug. You could forgive a man a lot who could do work like that. But it had to be Gilbert Sweet who had forged his signature and done those ringers, the Botticelli and the Piero di Cosimo. And their prove-nances? Why not? And his lovely, stolen Fra Angelico? No way, really, unless he'd done it when he was still at art school, or just left, because Anni delle Bandenere had given it away in 1953 and

Sweet only left the Gibby in '52. Which, you had to admit, made it possible, but only just.

What else did he know about those pictures? That the Piero di Cosimo didn't look quite right—the enchantment a shade contrived. That in the year in which Botticelli painted Messer Lorenzo—if he did—his sitter was ten years younger than the face on the panel. That the provenances were thin and suspect—a photocopy letter that turned out to be copied from one of Michelangelo's, and another from this Victorian geezer no one had heard of till Janey Bandenere flogged the pictures to Max Silverman. And Silverman had no ledger card for delle Bandenere, but did that mean anything? He could have weeded it, or bought through intermediaries. Doubt, all doubt, and still no certainty. Grrr!

He went through those weeks in a daze, haunted by the thought of his father filed hygienically till the law had done with him. On ice, literally. It was bad enough in court, hearing pathologists describe post-mortems; he'd never really got hardened to it. (The skull peeled like a fruit, opened like an egg, the organs . . .) The thought of his father like that made him shudder physically. A box of meat, bones, offal—the things they put in coffins. His own flesh and blood.

CHAPTER 19

HUNT

Balfour Road, too, was full of gloom; the children hated it in spite of the extra space, and indeed it seemed less roomy once they were there. Teresa wouldn't be able to work at Beak Street in the holidays and was bothered about old Nonna's ability to cope and afraid of eating her heart out in exile. And Corti was gloomy about other things besides his father. His lost picture, his lost career, his lost freedom to philander under his own roof. His money in the financial tide-rips with that eel Zappaterra. The growth-rate of the garden weeds. And having to pretend to go to work, because after a fortnight's suspension he still hadn't told them.

"I don't know, darling," he said to Teresa the evening after the vitriol trial. "I just don't know. I mean we do have more space here; it's healthier for the kids; they don't have to live surrounded by pushers and sex shops and that; they don't have the old folks trying to make them into little Eyeties, but . . . Oh, I just don't know."

"You're crazy, Franco. You change our name, now you change it back; you change our house and all our lives, and now you don't know! All those years, and at least I've had my work and my parents and my children. But no husband, Franco. You know who it is you married? Your stupid Metropolitan Police."

And she had married her Trattoria. That way it had worked, more or less, and for a policeman that was triumph, because the divorce rate in the Met was 80 per cent. And now the jobs they'd married were falling apart, and that was his fault, and . . .

Life wasn't going to be easy at Balfour Road.

He set off next morning for the Trattoria, collected his prints from Hector's microfilm, and, with Hector as guard-dog, settled down in the private dining alcove to write to Papworth.

URGENT, PERSONAL, AND CONFIDENTIAL.
Detective Chief Superintendent,
I understand you have evidence (meaning the typewriter specimen sheet) which could establish the source of the forged papers re the building-society account opened in my name.
I think that source is Maxwell Silverman. Previously reliable source has provided evidence that there are documents and works of art in his gallery which would incriminate him in this and other offences.

That was right. It was true enough but would suggest Informant Spadger, not Fiona. He couldn't use Hector's pictures; they'd want to know how he'd got them.

He listed Blamey's ledger card, the correspondence with Sweet, the carbon of the William Short letter, the sonnet "For AC"; the Rembrandt etchings, and finally his Fra Angelico.

Informant is closely connected with Maxwell Silverman International, but definitely not involved in crime, and has personally seen the above.

The last words were a lie. She hadn't. But she would back him, and if she didn't, well, the fortunes of war . . . He went on to spell out the implications. Blamey as murderer, Sweet's proven skills at forgery . . .

Taken together, hopefully this evidence justifies a search of the Silverman Gallery and, if confirmed, Silverman's arrest, also my own reinstatement.

Franco Corti (F. Short)
Detective Chief Inspector.

The change of name had just come through. It was a ray, like the evidence he'd given to the Guv. But he could do with one or two more.

He walked to the Yard and handed in the envelope without comment. Ten o'clock and a day to kill. The rain had moved away, leaving a lot of humidity behind, and July was ending under a hot, blistery sun. He sat down on a park bench and took his *Telegraph* from his briefcase. Automatically, his eye picked out the crime stories. A big murder trial up north, a kidnapping, a robbery or two. And—glory be to God! An arrest! Dermot Blamey, wanted in connection with the Harborough break-in; picked up in Liverpool by "Art and Antiques Squad detectives." He wondered how they'd got on to him, who'd gone up there, who'd do the questioning. How he'd react.

The thought of his enemy behind bars and himself the wrong side of a Berlin wall was acutely frustrating. An objective taken all right, an advance. But as long as he stayed outside, an advance in a different war.

Signing papers in Bruce Zappaterra's stifling office, with the windows shut against the racket of Mortimer Street, he hardly knew what he was doing.

That evening he phoned the Billingses and spoke to Jackie— Keith was working unsocial hours and would be back late.

"What's he working on then?"

"Blamey; he's over at Cannon Row with Mr. Wellow."

"When does Blamey come up for committal?"

"I'm not sure yet. Shall I let you know?"

"Please. And, Jackie—I handed in an envelope for the Guv this morning. About Silverman mostly. Some bits of evidence had come my way. . . ."

"Oh!"

"Oh what?"

"So that's where it came from. Yes, Mr. Hunt said there'd been a tip-off. He was going to get a warrant sworn out." Superintendent Neville Hunt, Deputy Guv, was the one who had been away on a course.

"Thank God. Did you know it's Silverman's been fitting me up? Did they say anything about that?"

"I don't know. Mr. Hunt's in charge. The Guv's off sick; there's a test match." Test matches had been known to give Papworth stomach pains. "I didn't see him. But Keithy did. I'll get him to ring . . ."

"No, not to worry. But if you could let me know when they've gone in . . ."

" 'Course we will, Mr. Short."

That was on a Friday. Four wet days followed, laden with doom and gloom, days of corrosive, unbearable boredom except for the time he could spend at home, and that was no pleasure. It wasn't till Tuesday morning that they rang.

"Shorty? Keith here. We've spun it." Spinning the drum means searching premises.

"Silverman?"

"Right."

"Did you pull him?"

"Not at home. Bit of a snafu, I'm afraid; he must have sussed us. They think he slipped out got up like an artist—false beard, dark glasses, portfolio—I mean, how corny can you get? They thought he was still inside. Got his wife, though, and another woman."

"Oh? Who's that, then?"

"Name of Rattray. The receptionist, do you remember?"

"Oh, *no!* But that's crazy! She's the one who . . . It was in my letter to the Guv. Who on earth did that?"

"Who d'you think? Hunt."

The stupid, bloody-minded berk! Typical! "What's he want to do a thing like that for?"

"Doesn't tell the peasants, does he?"

"Can't anyone make him change his mind? I mean the girl's honest as the day is long. What about Mr. Wellow? Would he talk to him, do you think?"

"He might if he was here, but he isn't; he's in South America. The Aztecs or something. Antiquities—you know—the great god Popocatapetl in solid gold, having a packet of babies for his tea. Something like that."

"Jackie then. Could she . . . ?"

"Fleas in both ears already. Ignorant interfering insubordinate schoolmarm, is my Jackie, and the Metropolitan Police does not appreciate petticoat government, thank you very much. She could have resigned, you know; she wasn't far off it."

"Poor old Jackie. Sounds as if that course hasn't improved Mr. Hunt."

"Well . . . Look, we're out of school, aren't we?"

"I am. Feel free, Keith."

"Well, then, our Nev's never exactly taken a small size in hats, and his head, now he's back . . . He needs a bleeding wheelbarrow for it. We're God's gift to poor old England, we are."

"And no ammo left—you and Jackie. Anyone else?"

"Can't think of anyone."

"I can't let this go, Keith. I'll have to have a try myself. Okay, so you pulled the two women. What else then?"

"I wasn't there myself, but according to Jackie, they found everything you said. Except Silverman, of course. And the cash; that'd gone. Oh yes, and there were some papers that must have been underneath it. She didn't get a look, but someone said they had your signature on them."

"My signature? But . . ."

"But you haven't written to him? I'll believe you."

He didn't like the sound of that: as if it might have gone the other way. Even Keith, even his friends . . .

And Silverman. All that effort, all that risk, and he walks out under their noses in a false beard!

After they rang off he sat for a long time cogitating about his approach. It was unavoidable. It would have to be the phone. He dialled the Yard, keyed up as an actor walking on stage. It wasn't too difficult getting Hunt on the phone. Then the flak started.

"Who's that? Corti? Short—whatever you call yourself? What the hell d'you think you're doing asking for me? Don't you know you're suspended from duty?" The voice was a terrier's bark, with overtones of the Officers' Mess—Hunt had done national service in the RAF and got a commission. "If you've any communication for me, put it in writing. . . ."

He must interrupt or the man would hang up on him. He picked his moment by instinct. "Mr. Hunt, sir; I know my position, and I hope I know my place, but this is urgent. I was hoping you'd let me see you."

Hunt yapped, "What?" so loud it hurt his eardrum.

"Yes, sir. I understand you're holding Miss Rattray from the Silverman, and . . ."

"It's none of your damned business who we're holding. Now look here, Short, I'm a busy man. So . . ."

"Mr. Hunt, sir. I do have some knowledge of this. I put you on to Silverman—and I promise you, Miss Rattray . . ."

"One of your women, is she?"

"Sir; you may be my senior in rank, but I must ask you not to insult my friends. I would like it, sir, if you would withdraw that innuendo." Bastard.

"And I would like it, Short, if you would bloody well remember who you're talking to. You've got a neck, by God. Oh, all right, perhaps I was a little hasty. But as for the Rattray woman . . ."

"She's on the level, sir. Honest. Straight as they come."

"Since when are you an authority on honesty, Chief Inspector?"

"Sir!" It was the only word he could find.

"When I require instruction in ethics, Chief Inspector, I shall go where they are observed, and when I wish for your advice about who is and who is not to be trusted, I shall ask for it. Meanwhile I'll have you know that under present circumstances any friend of yours will be accepted as honest only after full investigation."

"But . . ."

"I appreciate your wish to clear your name, and your willingness to sacrifice your associates to do so. . . ."

"*What* associates, if you please, sir?"

"Silverman."

"Associate! Silverman! An associate! I've been after that guy for twelve months or more. Ask Mr. Papworth, sir. He knew about my suspicions."

"Blank sheets of paper signed by you in his filing cabinet? My dear chap!"

"*What?!* Look, sir. I really ought to see you. I know who'll have done those; that guy Sweet—it's in my letter to the Guv. I can show you an example."

"When the evidence I already have has been properly studied. After that I'll think about it." After that, Titworth would be in charge again, thank God. After tonight, actually.

"And Miss Rattray, sir. You'll release her? I give you my word. . . ."

"I shall release Rattray if and when I'm satisfied there's no basis for charges. And as for your word—quite frankly, it wouldn't satisfy me of the time of day. Enough's enough, Short. Goodbye."

He ate his heart out for the rest of the day, rained off the streets to shelter in galleries, drifting into Butter Court and wondering what to do with the place, drinking whisky in bars. As soon as he could decently appear at home, he did so, adding to the general despondency. He had heartburn and his head ached, as if the only effect of the whisky had been a premature hangover. He waited till there might be a Billings at home, then rang.

"Anything new, Jackie?"

"Not really."

"Those two women still held?"

"'Fraid so. Oh yes—Blamey comes up for committal tomorrow."

"What charges? Just the Harborough job or anything else?"

"Just Harborough, I think."

"Any news of Silverman? Anyone know what made him run?"

"Not really. Unless . . . if he was mixed up with Blamey and . . . well, your father, like you wrote to the Guv . . . well, when Blamey was pulled . . ."

"Good thinking, Jackie. It might have been that. God, it's frustrating; when you think what that man's done . . . And you get all the evidence, hand him to the Guv on a plate, and they drop it! It makes you sick, Jackie, really sick. I tell you, much more of this, and I'll end up in hospital again."

"Don't do that, sir. It's always darkest before dawn. You'll win. Honest; everyone at A & A's sure you will."

Certainly there were glimmers. Silverman at large, but routed; it had to count as victory. Blamey in dead trouble, if not from him. As for Sweet—at first he hadn't had it in for Sweet like he had for the others, but now he wasn't so sure. Blank sheets with his signature on them? Okay, so the man was working for the spirits of the old masters, and in this day and age, with all this ESP research and that, who could say he wasn't? Sweet believed it, and he was daft enough for a clever guy like Silverman to exploit that and turn it to crime. Question: If a jury decides Botticelli used little Gilbert, then who's the artist? Gilbert's not responsible. And it's no crime for Botticelli to paint a Botticelli. "The legal standing of a ghost, m'lud?" The lawyers would have a ball.

Great. But when it came to signing *F. Short* on blank sheets of paper . . . No way that could be innocent. Craftsman or no craftsman, he'd see little Gilbert doing bird for that.

He was in court when Blamey came up for the Harborough job. As a spectator, naturally. No doubt about the identification; this was his man. The blue eyes defiant, a little mad, the skin curiously hard in texture. Corti allowed himself the luxury of gloating. When the prosecution got a remand in custody because further and more serious charges were being considered, he was cock-a-hoop.

He came out of court about four, into hot, showery weather with a threat of thunder, caught a bus to Knightsbridge to kill time, and bought an evening paper to read in the park.

He sat down listlessly and started on the crime stories. CAMPUS DOPE SCANDAL. PROFESSOR CHARGED. *Mamma mia!* Gervase Willison! They'd been sniffing cocaine by the yard! He couldn't say he was surprised; that weirdo could be into anything. Remember his eyes that first time? Was that it? Was he stoned?

Because if he was . . . And he was, I swear it! The way he kept caricaturing himself and going all wild and ecstatic. Stoned to the eyeballs, walking around all euphoric with his head in a golden cloud. He'd have believed me if I'd said the front cover of *Men Only* was a Fra Angelico. So . . . ?

So sod it to hell and back to square bleeding one, and no more clue about that painting than the first time I saw it.

Showers and bright intervals. Better than the trough of gloom.

Keeps you on your toes. Keeps you dancing. Hail sweeping in across Kensington had him sprinting like a rabbit.

The next bright interval looked more permanent. It started with a phone call from the Guv. "Chief Inspector Corti? Report for duty oh-eight-thirty tomorrow. And don't be bloody late."

CHAPTER 20

BAR THE SHOUTING

He felt awkward, the way they all stared or didn't, and the Guv's way of putting him at ease was predictably quaint. England had won the test, with Boycott the hero of the match, or it could have been quainter.

"Right. Here's your warrant card. And happen you'll do me a favour and stop out of trouble. There's thieves to be caught, lad; I've sufficient work and more without wasting time on my officers' private bloody shenanigans."

"Yes, sir. Thank you for getting me reinstated, sir. That was quick work, if I may say so." A thing like that could drag on for a year, though not perhaps in face of cast-iron evidence of a stitch-up.

"Very fair-minded officers at CIB. So I told 'em straight, I showed 'em the evidence; they agreed; and we went up and got clearance on the spot."

"Thank you very much, sir."

"There's no call to repeat yourself. Now then, this Silverman. You'd a deal of evidence. I'd not expect that from an officer under suspension. How did you get it?"

He was ready for that. "Information received, sir."

"Oh aye?"

"And . . . well, Guv, having to leave here quick and that, it must have upset me. I seem to have left General Orders behind."

"Oh aye? Very good, Shorty. I'll not press."

"Can I talk to Mrs. Silverman?"

"I'll not stop you. Nothing else then? Right; you can go. And take your property with you; it's not wanted here."

"My property, Guv?"

"Don't be bloody daft, lad. Your picture. Tempera on panel, Florentine school. Sign here." He felt like a lover reunited with his love.

Half an hour later, sad as a lover saying goodbye, he handed it in at his bank.

What now? Tie in the loose ends. Sweet. The phoney Botticelli, the phoney Piero di Cosimo still without proof. Peace to be made with Fiona, whom the Guv had released as soon as he got back to work. He headed for the Silverman Gallery, taking pleasure from an encounter with Neville Hunt in the corridor.

"Corti—it is Corti, is it, not Short? I'm afraid I owe you an apology. . . ."

He said, "Do you, sir?" and went on his way.

At the gallery it was worse than he expected. Fiona wouldn't speak to him, wouldn't meet his eye, but turned her back and walked off. He followed her, protesting, as far as the door of the loo, and she slammed it in his face. He waited till she came out and told her the whole story.

She didn't much like it, but she saw the point. If she'd known he was suspended, she'd have been an accessory. She accepted that it wasn't him who'd had her nicked. She even agreed to lie for him and say she'd seen all the incriminating papers.

But she couldn't stomach Elsa Silverman being held. "It's indecent. She's as innocent as I am. She's suffering enough as it is. I mean, who's going to cope? We can't sign the cheques, we can't do a thing. I'll have to close the gallery, and the porter-packer hasn't had his wages. And her house, poor woman . . ."

He left without kissing her. He had a feeling that subject was closed.

Elsa Silverman took it better. She was in her own clothes and wearing make-up; expecting to be let out any minute. He wasn't so sure about that. He was sorry for her and he didn't think she was involved, but holding her was the one thing that could bring friend Max home. Details like her guilt or innocence would have to wait. They wouldn't let Elsa go till they had to.

But now it was resignation, and anger at her husband. She swore he never told her a thing. Not even that he was leaving, and Jackie Billings confirmed that later, because she'd been there and had seen Elsa go to look for him and come back shattered. "It's the end of my marriage, Chief Inspector, I can tell you."

"I'm sorry. I really am. It's always the women who get hurt; they never think of that. Where's he gone then? Brazil?" He'd skimmed through her statement and she'd suggested it.

"Only guesswork. But São Paolo's doing so well, and the woman who runs it for him—I've often wondered . . . And getting people out of there—I mean, look at Biggs." Her voice was improved without its exaggerated upper-class bray.

There had been nothing in the statement about the Korndorffer pictures, so he asked, "You don't happen to know where your husband got them?"

She knew them. "But where they came from? The West Country, I think. Would it be Worcestershire, somewhere in Worcestershire?"

Birds began singing in his head. "Not Monte Carlo then? Someone mentioned Count Bandenere."

"I don't think so. Max did have some correspondence with him—about a Fra Angelico or something, but . . . Look, I think we had an old inventory of the Bandenere collection, late Victorian. I expect your people will have found it."

They hadn't, and Corti couldn't trace a copy. But she was right about São Paolo and the manageress; it took a month to confirm it, and not much longer to find out that, just like Biggs the train robber, Silverman had a child there and couldn't be extradited.

Bob Wellow yawned enormously. "Sorry, Shorty. Touch of the old jet-lag. It's not so bad, you know, losing Silverman like that. It's a rotten climate; he can never come home again; his wife, his home . . . I reckon he'll feel he's being punished even if you don't."

"Perhaps you're right. He certainly adored that old bag, whatever he'd got on the side."

"And as for the Rattray girl; couple of nights in the nick? She's young; she'll get over it. Dine out on it for the rest of her life, I shouldn't wonder. Don't give it another thought, old man. How's the old ticker making out?"

"Hadn't really thought about it." That wasn't quite true, because of that moment in the Silverman Gallery, when suddenly there was his Fra Angelico (correction: his alleged Fra Angelico), but apart from that . . . "D'you know, that doc could have been right. It's helped a lot, getting Frank Short and that out of my system."

"I'm glad to hear it. Well" —Bob looked at his watch— "I might be able to lend a hand myself. In ten minutes' time I've an appointment with a gent called Blamey to talk about your old dad. We'll see what I can get out of him, shall we?"

But no way could Corti get within a mile of Blamey, which was sensible of the Guv, or he'd probably have broken his neck.

The bits were falling into place. In spite of Silverman he felt a qualified happiness. By any standards friend Max had taken a beating. Fiona? He shrugged. Too bad. Blamey? Wait and see. There was unfinished business on the Zappaterra front, and with Gilbert Sweet, but what increasingly filled his mind was his family. The children still hated Balfour Road (fitted up now with its alarm system) and didn't like being little Shorts, which they weren't, any more than he liked being a big one.

"Clear out?" he asked Teresa that night. "Old folks at home? Back to the Trattoria?"

She looked at him for a long time, then said, "Does it have to be the Trattoria? Somewhere nearer perhaps, but . . ."

Suddenly it was staring him in the face. He jumped up and spread his hands in a fine Italian gesture. "Butter Court! Why not Butter Court? Quiet little street; we'd have to do it up, of course, and I wouldn't stint you. . . ."

"Oh, Franco! *Yes!* A thousand times yes!"

"So what are we waiting for? Let's tell the kids."

That night it was good in bed, and next day he put 23 Balfour Road up for sale.

He was nearly his old self. He strode confidently into the Yard for a day's catching up before he tackled little Gilbert. If there were any stares or nudges today, he didn't see them. Bob Wellow was out questioning Blamey again. He had the office to himself, and the heaps of papers shrank satisfactorily. He had been at it for an hour when in walked Chuck Carrozza.

Eyebrows, knife-edge slacks, tweedier-than-tweed jacket, shoulders as broad as his own. "Hi, Shorty!"

"Chuck!" It was like shaking hands with a monkey-wrench. "I thought you were back in Washington."

"I was, but I got diamond business. Antwerp, Amsterdam, maybe Hatton Garden. Well, what's new around here? How's your poppa? Any more handouts?"

All'Italiana, Franco. Keep your cool.

He said very quietly, "Only under his will."

"Oh, *no!* You don't say? Gee, I'm sorry. Guess I opened my big mouth once too often. How'd it happen?"

The tale had to be told, or as much as was fit for police ears. It needed delicacy. Carrozza mustn't think his father was bent or he'd been shielding him or anything. He'd had the same problem with the Guv, and he thought he'd got away with it.

But not with another Italian. He sensed the man's mind working: supplying the unsaid, assuming the worst; assuming he was bent himself. When he had finished he waited a few seconds and said softly, "No, Chuck. You've got it wrong. Not me. You'd see why if you knew old Sargey."

Carrozza seemed not to hear, and Corti knew he'd at least implanted a doubt. After a few moments' silence he said, "Right, Chuck. Nice to see you. Now if you'll excuse me . . ."

"Hold it. You remember those pictures of old Korndorffer's? The Botticelli and the other one?"

"The one as was sensitive."

"Yeah. Well, I got news. Busby said to give it to you. Take a look at this."

It was a carbon of a letter dated 5th January, 1980, and addressed to Mr. Maxwell Silverman at Duke Street.

Sir,

An 1878 inventory of the Bandenere pictures has come into my possession. I searched it in vain for the Botticelli portrait and the di Cosimo *Diana* which I purchased on your assurance, supported by documents, that the Bandeneres had owned them since they were painted.

Sir, you are a crook. You have used forged papers to sell me fakes. Having neither my youth nor my health, I must forgo the pleasure of beating the living daylights out of you and have recourse instead to the law.

If you wish to escape this, you may send me your proposals for reparation. In their absence or inadequacy I shall inform the police one month from today.

Contemptuously,
Sampson Grenfell Korndorffer.

Corti read it twice, then nodded gravely. "Thanks. Though whether the courts would accept that as evidence . . ."

"Right. What about this then?" A book came out of a pocket, bound in green leather with a black-striped shield (Bandenere means Blackbands) surrounded by gilt curlicues. Inside, dated and superbly handwritten, was the inventory itself.

"No Botticelli?" Corti asked. "No Piero di Cosimo?"

"Nope."

"Wraps it up then, doesn't it?"

"Sure does."

"Where the hell did you get it?"

"New York City Police. It seems old Korndorffer died with this business unfinished. His family suppressed it so they could get good prices. Wouldn't know how the cops got on to it; I'm just the leg-man. Maybe one or two other things stank."

"But this is great, Chuck. Really great."

"Glad to be of service. Any time."

Corti thought, Personally. He thinks this helps me personally. Those words from a fellow-Italian could mean, You owe me for this, pal, and don't you forget it.

Old Bob got back in mid-afternoon, clapped out, to chuck an unsealed envelope on Corti's desk. He drew out the folded sheets of typescript, not daring to hope. But it was definitely a statement and definitely signed D. I. Blamey.

And then he didn't need to hope. There it was. The works. How Bob did it he'd never know, but that Scouse had sung like Pavarotti. One of those very rare cases, the villain who flips and truly and honestly repents his sins. . . .

Yes, he had, inter alia, nicked Lord Harborough's tin; he'd procured Arthur Gudgeon to stop Madame Verdier's mouth; he'd conspired with Maxwell Silverman to steal this picture and broken into 23 Balfour Road and done it. And finally—and he was going to roast in hell for this; there it was in black and white over his signature—he had sent Antonio Corti a warning about grassing, and later, when Maxwell Silverman started dropping hints (no; he couldn't swear he'd put it to him straight), he had plucked up courage and gone to Butter Court and killed.

Reading it, Corti felt an unfamiliar sensation all over his face, and it dawned on him that for the first time for a week he was smiling.

CHAPTER 21

AN EMPTY GUN

One enemy taken, one routed. That left Sweet. He couldn't resent that man like he did the others, but he had his job to do.

Next morning he left for Worcestershire with a warrant in his pocket and Jackie Nunn beside him because of Dorothy Horse-Face. He drove without hurrying, without much talk, under greying skies. On the Oxford ring road he had to turn on his wipers; by Burford it was headlights and up into mist; thunder drummed them off the Cotswolds and they crossed the invisible Severn in a downpour.

Beyond Upton the rain was tremendous; there was a time when the wipers couldn't cope and they had to pull in and sit damply with the windows steamed up, while water infiltrated the coachwork. It was pouring, though no longer at monsoon strength, when he stopped at the foot of Hare Hill and wound the window down to look. The track was muddy and its ruts miniature torrents, but at least it didn't smell. Sweet's Range Rover would have a job getting up today, and for the car it was out of the question.

"Cor!" he said. "We'll be soaked. Did you bring a mac?" She had, efficient girl. It'd have to be some mac to stop that lot. He'd been too preoccupied himself. He was soaked within fifty yards.

On top, you felt the wind. The rain gusted and swirled round the cottage, mingled with cloud that made the place an island.

An island off the coast of life, and they were swimming towards it. The door was locked, and no one answered his hammering. Hm. The Range Rover was there, so Sweet must be at home. You wouldn't expect the door to be locked in daytime, not in the country. He wondered whether to break it down. Instead, he squelched his way to the studio and looked in. Through the whoosh and rattle on the slates he could hear an orchestra at full blast, with women screeching their heads off. The "Ride of the Valkyries" or something. The stove, open, alight and infinitely desirable, beckoned him in, and in front of it on the rugs Gilbert Sweet and his woman lay with their backs to him, enjoying their quadraphonic shindy.

He got them to hear by tapping with a coin during a lull in the music. Sweet got up, looking surly, and nodded towards him—probably couldn't see who it was through the streaming glass—and Corti went back to the door.

It duly opened, but cautiously and only a few inches, revealing Gilbert Sweet's maned head with its bare white crown. Revealing also, like a miniature spectacle frame, the twin muzzles of his shotgun.

Fear gave him a few seconds' grace before it pounced. He said, "Morning, Mr. Sweet. Filthy weather we're having. You remember me—John Marovitz, Black Lion. This is my partner, Mrs. Nunn. Can we come in, please?"

"Now." That didn't mean now, it meant no.

"But— We're soaked to the skin, dammit. . . ."

"Can't come in here."

"Look, I've got a proposition for you. You remember, we were talking about—"

"Gow away." The gun rose and swivelled till it was a foot from his private parts, and it was then that the panic shot through him, like with a near-miss in a car, when you don't start trembling till the danger is past. Only this time it was just beginning.

It took all his will and training not to show it; at least he hoped he didn't. "Oh, come on, Mr. Sweet; put it down. That won't do you any good, you know."

Sweet smiled then. "Wown't do *you* any good, mister, not if it gows off." Corti saw how mad he was and hesitated, judging distance, conscious of Valkyrie hysterics in the studio, of water trickling down the small of his back. Not close enough. Not safe to move in.

"Gow awye!" Sweet sounded petrified too. "Gow on. Get out!"

"But why, what . . . ?" It was superfluous; the guy mightn't want to do business with John Marovitz, but he wouldn't take a gun to him.

"Why? You're a liar, that's why. You're not John Marovitz. You're the police. Gow awye."

"Now what gave you that idea? . . ."

"Asked my dealer, didn't I? Black Lion Gallery fowlded. Marovitz not around."

"But—"

"Look, he knows you. Phowned me, didn't he, to ask what you looked like. You're Mr. Short, that's who you are."

The fear was giving way to fury, directed mostly at himself. Sussed every time! Algernon (Papworth's predecessor) was right again: "Corti, if you want to play silly buggers with disguises, you need a forgettable face." And a matter arising as well. Sweet tells Silverman: That's all friend Maxie needs. Friend Maxie takes off. His own stupid fault. Grrr!

"Now gow away. I'm gowing to count to ten . . ." The Valkyries' war-whoop stormed down the narrow hall on the backs of the brass. ". . . three, four . . ."

"Gilbert!" A sharp, frightened voice tagged on to the Valkyries. "Gilbert! Put that thing down! What on earth do you think you're doing? Who is it? Put that thing down and let him in." Horse-Face; thank God for Horse-Face.

Sweet took no notice ". . . five, six . . ."

Cool it. How? Change the subject. "That's interesting, Mr. Sweet, about Max Silverman. That is the one, is it? Your dealer?"

At least it interrupted the counting. "What's that got to do with you? Why shouldn't it be him?"

"Just I thought you might like to know—he's gone. Brazil, I expect. You'll have to find a new outlet, because I don't think he'll be back."

That was probably the point where reality broke through and Sweet knew he'd had it. The little features contracted and seemed to whiten. A new runnel had opened up near Corti's armpit, and he couldn't stop shivering. Frenzied Wagnerian yodels sawed at his eardrums. What it must sound like inside that room! . . .

Reality may have got through to Gilbert Sweet, but not for long, because with no more warning than that change in expression, he began to clown. He threw his door open and bowed like a courtier from Queen Elizabeth on the telly, with an upward sweep of his arm. But he kept hold of his gun.

"Mr. Short and Mrs. Nunn. Shorty and Nunny, Nunny and Shorty. My humble abode lies, be it never so humble, at your feet. Pray enter, good gentles. Ow, I say! You're ever so wet." He giggled. "You'd better take your clothes off, didn't you? Ow, do, we're men of the world here, aren't we, Doll? Doll's ever such a man of the world. She'll help you. She'd like that, Doll would. P'raps she'll undress too. Let's all undress Doll. Would that be nice, Nunny? Shorty thinks it would. . . ." The speech went on with the bowings and caperings of a court jester, drowned intermittently by the Valkyries, and Corti, thinking only of that gun and how to get hold of it, saw that Gilbert wasn't going to let him.

They were in the hall now. Outside, it was getting lighter and the rain was easing. In the far doorway Sweet's woman drooped, sexless and round-shouldered, silhouetted against the studio crimson. Corti searched his mind for gambits. Bob Wellow would know what to say, but you couldn't exactly ring him and ask. Between himself and Doll, Gilbert had adopted a tough Western slouch, with his gun in one hand like a pistol, butt under his arm. "Howdy, Sheriff; yuh gonna come 'n'git me, or are yuh plumb yaller? Know sumpin', Sheriff? No one comes and gits Two-Gun Gil, but no one. Cos yer yaller, the whole goldarned bunch of yuh, an' Two-Gun Gil's gonna count to ten an' then he's gonna shoot yuh dead. So git prayin', mister. On your knees. You too, ma'am. Gow on. Down . . ."

Before Corti could make his mind up what to do, the picture changed and Gilbert was in the SS with a stage German accent. "Schweinhund! Englisch Schweinbund! Talk! I haf ways of making you talk. . . ." After that he was Al Capone, then Kojak, then the IRA, and after that he ran out of ideas and sat crosslegged on the floor with the gun aimed at Corti's belly.

The Valkyries had calmed down too. Doll's voice, expressionless, cut into the comparative quiet. "It isn't loaded, you know. He hasn't got any cartridges."

"Ow yass, it is!" He was Gilbert Sweet again, and angry. "You shut up or I'll show you just how lowded it is." Was that fantasy too? Probably, but you wouldn't take the risk.

"It isn't, actually. But it doesn't make any difference; he wouldn't have the guts to use it. I shouldn't take any notice if I were you . . ." Her voice was utterly lifeless.

"You bitch! You bitch, you cow, you . . . You shut up or I'll shoot right up your nasty . . ." He was screaming, and his language was filthy. You could tell from the way he used it he didn't often talk like that. For an instant he turned, but Corti, stiff and cold and shivering, was too slow, and before he had moved, the gun was back on him.

"Down't you come near me! It's lowded. Promise. Makes a nasty wound, does a shotgun; very nasty indeed."

He didn't need Sweet to tell him that. God, he was cold! His fingers and toes were numb, and his teeth hadn't stopped chattering since he got there.

Behind Gilbert Sweet, Doll, propped in her doorway, shook her head and frowned, and he understood that Jackie Billings, behind him, must be making signs at her. Encouraging her to have a go?

"No," he said quietly, hoping Sweet wouldn't hear because of the Valkyries. "No, Jackie."

And then there was a commotion, and Sweet had raised his gun and he dived at Sweet's ankles and fell short, and he lay waiting for death and thinking, No Valkyries to cart me to Valhalla, only God and his holy Mother, and he started to say a Hail Mary. . . .

"She's gone round outside, Gilbert," said Doll. "She'll creep up behind you with her handcuffs, and after that I'll probably kick your useless bloody balls."

Corti got up.

Sweet had gone quiet, his face white and haggard, not knowing which way to look. Behind poor Doll, Wagner was fairly whooping it up. The noise was terrific. He shouted, "Leave it alone, Gilbert. Come on, give us that gun; then we can all talk reasonably."

"*Heyaha!*" yelled Helmwige, Gerhilde, Siegrune, and Grimgerde, forte fortissimo. "*Hoyotoho! Heyaha!*" Screeched Ortlinde, Rossweisse, Schwertleite, and Waltraute. "*Heyaha!*"

Jackie was in the studio by now; he watched her approach Doll carefully from behind, and saw Doll start and then produce something that in a pinch you could call a smile.

Must keep the man's attention. He risked it and stood up, painfully, stiff with cold.

"Come on, Gilbert. You're really not helping yourself or anyone. . . ."

"*Hoyotoho! Hoyotoho! Heyaha!*"

Gilbert grinned. It was a very innocent grin. "Fooled you, didn't I? 'Course it isn't loaded. Look." He put on a ham actor's voice. "I die! Farewell! I die!" He sniggered, put the muzzle in his mouth, and blew two thirds of his head off.

Time and space closed in. There was nothing outside Corti any more. No world. No past. No future. His eyelids were jammed shut, his ears out of action. His universe was himself and his body and their conflict. His body roared at him and wouldn't stop shaking and was desperate to jettison its contents, and he was fighting it with all his strength to hold the spincters, reconquer the limbs, then at last get his eyes open and look.

His universe took in the death and the redness. It expanded to include the smell, then the music ending and Doll howling in Jackie's arms and bits of Gilbert Sweet's face stuck to his own. Thoughts began to form. Why him, for Jesus' sake? Why not that twisted murdering Scouse? Or even bloody Silverman? And that woman. Why? It's always the women who suffer. Poor cow.

He found the telephone and made his fingers dial 999.

It would be a few minutes before they came, and Jackie had taken Doll to clean herself up. He walked out onto Hare Hill.

The rain had moved on and hung from enormous gleaming clouds in indigo curtains. He stood in the long wet grass and shivered. Sounds got through to him. Cattle, a lorry, an excited dog. A lark high up, singing its heart out. Numbly he registered that the view was spectacular, and as he watched, a rainbow arched from Upton on Severn spire to Bredon Hill and the numbness ran together in his throat.

Sunshine clapped him on the back. He took his coat off to let in the warmth. The fields steamed and glittered, and there was a hope that somewhere, someday, life could be endurable again.